POZ

The Lives of Remy and
Michael, Book One

C. Koehler

A NineStar Press Publication

www.ninestarpress.com

Poz

Printed in the USA

ISBN: 978-1-64890-201-7

NineStar Edition, January, 2021
Originally Published in January 2015

Also available in eBook, ISBN: 978-1-64890-200-0

WARNING:

This book contains sexual content, which may only be suitable for mature readers, the death of a minor character, and homophobic slurs.

Even at an allegedly gay-friendly high school, being out isn't easy, not if you play a sport. Remy didn't just play a sport, he lived for a sport. He bled crew and rowed with his best friend, Mikey. He'd known him forever but was a year ahead of him in school and crew, varsity to his JV. But then something changed. They were on the way to a regatta in San Diego and suddenly they noticed each other. Remy don't know what happened. They'd changed in front of each other in the locker rooms all the time at school. But Remy'd never looked and suddenly all he could do was stare.

Remy thought Mikey felt the same, yet somehow Mikey didn't want a relationship. Whatever, Remy didn't have time for drama. They had a major regatta to prepare for. They make apps to help lonely young men to find temporary companionship, and let's just say, Remy enjoyed the summer before his senior year. Then everything caught up with him and it all came apart.

Mikey was furious, but if he didn't want a relationship, why was he angry? It turned out there was a price for playing around, and when Remy got sick, he had to wonder, where would Mikey be?

Poz is dedicated to the memory of Spencer Cox (March 10, 1968—December 18, 2012).

Spencer worked tirelessly as a member of ACT UP throughout the worst years of the AIDS epidemic to effect change and further advances in HIV treatment, working with the FDA to speed the approval of HIV medications, including the then-new class, protease inhibitors, which revolutionized the treatment of HIV. You can learn more about Spencer's contributions in How to Survive A Plague (2012).

When I knew Spencer, I didn't know he was a hero.

Prologue

APRIL
My senior year

"Hey, Remy," Michael said as he walked up. "Coach says hands-on in fifteen."

I looked up at my guy. The warm San Diego sun shone behind his head, giving him a halo to match the one I always saw when I looked at him, at least now. I can't believe there was a time I couldn't see how amazing he was. I smiled at him. I couldn't help it. I tipped my head up, and he obliged. I lost myself in his kiss, my eyes closing as his lips brushed against mine, softly at first but with increasing ardor. He knelt next to where I sat, driving all thoughts of my homework right out of my mind as he held my face lightly.

"All right, you two. Get a hotel."

We broke apart, foreheads touching and cheeks blazing. "Sorry, Howie," I said.

Our cox'n rolled his eyes. "You two are so sickeningly sweet together, I can feel cavities developing. At least I know you'll be relaxed and won't rush the slide."

"It's not like I nailed him in the bathroom," Michael said dryly.

"As hot as that visual is, I need you two to bring oars down to the beach. Then wait by the boat," Howie said. "I have to go herd the rest of the squirrels."

We each grabbed four oars and headed back down to the beach. We weren't supposed to carry that many at a time, and if Coach Lodestone caught us, he'd huff and he'd puff and he'd threaten to blow the house down, but one of the things I'd learned over the last year was that his bark was far worse than his bite. Mostly he would grouse that we'd scratch the paint on the blades of the oars, but we were careful, Michael and I.

After we set the oars against the slings holding the boat, we scampered back up to where we'd stashed our gear, and never mind what Howie said about waiting by the boat. I'm on a fearsome cocktail of drugs, and I needed more sunblock before I was on the water. Naturally, Michael helped with those hard-to-reach places, like that spot right between my shoulder blades where my unisuit always managed to gape. I really didn't want to take chances with a burn. The Crew Classic only had two kinds of weather: rainy and miserable or sunny and hot. Fortune favored us this year. It was sunny. During rainy years, boats sometimes filled with so much water they had to be pulled from the chop by the Coast Guard. Rowing shells were meant to keep water out, not hold it in. Crew

Classic legend held that after one particularly bad year, a crew was forced to abandon ship right in the middle of Mission Bay. The cox'n, who was last aboard, stood in her seat and bowed to the referees' tent and the jumbotron cameras before executing a perfect dive into the chop. Then the safety launch plucked her from the water. That was cox'ns for you.

Sunblock applied, we still managed to be back at the boat before Howie returned to our knot of rowers with the last of the stragglers. So did Coach Lodestone.

"Nice of you to join us, gentlemen." Coach Lodestone looked over his sunglasses at the laggards as they joined our cluster. "I trust you didn't make Howie look too hard for you."

"No, sir."

"Good, good, because I'd hate to inconvenience anyone by requiring punctuality for this race, the last of their high school careers for five of your boatmates." Once he was sure he had their full attention, he continued. "This has been a good season for this lineup. Yes, we had some issues last fall, but head racing has never been our focus, and I think this spring has helped us—you—click as a crew. The weather is amazing, some of the best I've ever seen as a rower or as a coach. This is it. Make the most of it, and most of all, enjoy it."

Coach Lodestone put his hand in the middle of the cluster. Nine other hands swiftly followed his. "The worst thing is to cross the finish line with regrets, so make yourselves proud, because I'm proud of you."

"All right, enough chitchat," Howie barked. "Find your places aaand hands-on! Ready...aaand up to shoulders! We're rowing the *Helena Sundstrom* today. It's a solid boat, so try not to suck."

The junior crew of the Capital City Rowing Club had bought it off CalPac College last fall. It was no longer stiff enough for collegiate competition but still had plenty of life left in it, and we were lucky to have it.

The weather might have been perfect, but the water of Mission Bay still had a chill in it, pleasant in the heat of the afternoon. We waded out until we were knee-deep so we wouldn't scrape the boat on the sand when we climbed in. We took our oars from the junior varsity rowers who had kindly volunteered to bring them to us.

"Bow pair in!" Howie called from the shallows once all the oars were in their oarlocks. The oars acted like outriggers, lending a certain stability to the boat. It wasn't easy to roll an eight, but it could be done.

"Engine room, climb in." The four rowers in the middle of the boat clamored in. That figured. They were meat that moved the boat, but could they not climb in without the racket? Just once?

"Seven, your turn! Hold it steady, bow six. We'll tie in once we're on the water. Stroke, if you'd be so kind?"

He meant me. Howie was tiny. He was the only one who could see where we were going, but he brought no power to the boat. He was supposed to be small. That said, this race standardized cox'ns' weights. He had to carry a sandbag to bring him up to the minimum weight, and to prevent any cheating, race officials weighed all sandbags at the end of the race. What? Cox'ns bleeding sand out during the course of a race to give their crews an advantage? If they thought they could have gotten away with it.

So, while we rowers might've been knee-deep in the water, Howie was waist-deep. I carried him from the shallows and set him in the boat's stern. He fiddled with his cox box, the small device that counted strokes and powered the boat's sound system.

"Your turn, Remy."

I climbed in last. Stroke didn't have to be superstrong. I just had to hold a beat and not allow myself to be rushed by the seven people sitting behind me. I wouldn't be, and I knew I had seven great rowers behind me, Michael among them at seven. Together we made the stroke pair, and did we ever take flack for that.

All traces of his snarkiness gone, Howie started issuing commands as the *Helena* pulled away from the beach. From now until the boat was washed and back in slings after the race, his word was law. It might sound silly or mystical, but I already felt the power coursing through the carbon fiber of the oars and the shell. It was Howie's job to remind us how we rowed for the next thirty minutes of our warm-up and race, and he was brilliant at it. Soon we would click, eight bodies moving as one under the guidance of Howie's voice, the oars creaking as we pulled them through the water, bending under the strain of our bodies.

My last thought as we sat at the ready, waiting for the countdown, Sea World in the background, was that I'd almost thrown all of this away.

We were in San Diego at the Crew Classic, the last and biggest race of my rowing career with the juniors program of the Capital City Rowing Club. It was the end of my senior year of high school, and everything was golden. It would become one of my favorite memories.

It wasn't always like that. At one point during the previous year, I had doubted I would make it, and I don't mean qualifying for a seat in a boat for San Diego. I didn't say things like that out loud anymore because everyone told me I was melodramatic, and maybe I was. But that didn't change the fact that it was true. I wasn't entirely out my junior year, and I made a lot of stupid decisions that hurt a lot of people, most especially myself. I hurt Michael and my brother, too, and I didn't think I would be able to make it up to them anytime soon. Or maybe I wouldn't have to. They seemed to have forgiven me.

I still had to forgive myself.

This was something I struggled with every day.

Chapter One

APPROXIMATELY ONE YEAR EARLIER
The end of my junior year

When all this started, my older brother Geoff didn't know I was gay, at least not to my knowledge. I'd called him "Goff" when we were really young because I couldn't pronounce his name. He'd called me "Germy" because he couldn't say Jeremy. He still calls me Germy, even though everyone else calls me Remy. I still called him Goff, so I guess that was fair.

Goff was thirteen minutes older—we were twins of the fraternal variety—and he milked that older bit like a Holstein cow. Thirteen minutes, but you would have thought it was thirteen years. Anyway, he played football. He looked out for me, or at least tried, but he was and is straight as a plank. We wrangled a lot, still do, but he saved me from a lot of homophobic hassling, sometimes at the hands of his own friends, without even knowing I was gay, which was pretty cool of him.

"Teammates," Goff would say. "They're not my friends, not if they're giving you shit."

He was a good guy when he wasn't being an asshole.

That said, Goff never understood a fundamental part of me, at least not until I came out to him. I guess that was my fault though. How could he when I'd never told him I was gay? But how could I when I couldn't have borne losing my brother? He was my twin, the person I was closest to in the world. Losing him would've meant losing a part of me. We fought like cats in a gunnysack and it drove our parents crazy, but they never understood that we went to the trouble of irritating one another because we loved one another. We certainly weren't going to tell one another that. We were (and are) teenage males. Dad was a shrink. Dr. Babcock should've gotten that but didn't.

So anyway, Goff missed a major piece of who I was and everything that went along with it. Now I wouldn't say all teenage boys were sex-obsessed, just every one I've ever encountered. But he had all the sex he wanted and had no idea what it's like not getting it. For me, it was not being gotten. So, I was horny as hell in high school and about to burst. That was the start of all my problems, I guess.

Our family lived in Davis, an über-liberal organogroovy college town about seventy miles from San Francisco. Davis had bought into Cesar Chavez's grape boycott, which I read about in history class; it made itself a nuclear-free zone, which was kind of a joke when UC Davis boasted a particle accelerator of its very own. Besides, what good would the declaration of being a nuclear-free zone have done? Protect the city if the US and the USSR had nuked each other? There were three major Air Force bases around the city during the Cold War. There'd have been a bright-blue flash and then nothing. Good luck with that nuclear-free zone. The city was also a declared sanctuary for undocumented immigrants. I could go on, but why bother? A homecoming prince even brought his boyfriend to prom one year. As a gay kid, I should've been golden in a city and high school like this.

But someone forgot to send my parents that memo, or at least my mother. Mom was a smart woman—she majored in chemistry in college and went on to become a drug rep for a pharmaceutical company after she decided getting a PharmD wasn't for her—but she was oblivious sometimes, especially where Goff and I were concerned. Of both our parents, she was the louder with the compulsory heterosexuality messaging, things like telling me I was morally obligated to take some unpopular (read: fat with braces) girl to the prom. She said it was my "gentlemanly duty" or some such bull, but Goff and I both knew it was because she herself had been fat with braces in high school. She wasn't doing it deliberately—trying to make me miserable—but she succeeded admirably.

Women in Mississippi had taken their girlfriends to prom, or at least tried. Hell, even in Davis a few years ago, the aforementioned homecoming prince took his boyfriend, but my mom? She thought I had to make life better for every desperate and dateless girl out there, just to restore some cosmic balance because her life sucked during high school. Why didn't she get that this was my life, my one-way ticket through high school, not her do-over?

When I said things like that, her response was, "I think you can take one evening out of your life to make a difference in someone else's." Given the essentially obligatory service hours necessary to get into college these days, I thought I already had.

My boyfriend could've plowed me on the table at Thanksgiving, and she would have still said that. If I'd had a boyfriend. Well, there was Mikey Castelreigh. He wanted to be my boyfriend. I thought of him more as a kid brother even though he was only a year younger. I felt like there was a big difference between a sophomore and a junior in high school, however. Mikey looked like he missed the puberty train. I had a left hand. What I needed was a close friend who was gay. Mikey fit that bill very well.

Even at good ol' tolerant, GSA-sporting Davis High, it wasn't easy being different. We were still teenagers. Being smacked on the ass with the gay wand when I was born didn't change that. I wanted to think Mikey understood that. I think what Mikey didn't get was why we couldn't be friends with benefits. Uh...because it would have been like blowing my brother? If I had a brother who swung that way. But then, as has been pointed out to me many times, I also saw what I wanted to see and not always what was really there. Or boats. I saw rowing-related things very clearly. It was life that tripped me up at every turn.

But telling my parents? Like that would ever happen. Hear that flapping noise? That was the pigs flying out of my butt, which would happen right before I'd tell my parents I liked the cock. I never got the best vibe off them where that was concerned. Sure, they had gay and lesbian, even trans, friends, but it was different when it was their kid, you know? They were on a need-to-know basis where my life was concerned. Coming out? Survey says: No!

Goff told our parents about a lot of things that went on his life—whereas I told them very little—but then he and I had very different relationships with them.

"So how's that working for you, Goff?"

"Shut it."

I smiled, but it was really more of a smirk. "Still think having the olds know every single detail's harmless?"

"You're really kind of a dick sometimes, you know that?"

"Everybody has to be something, I guess."

"Really? I thought you were more of an asshole."

He had no idea what he was doing to me with this conversation. I mean, the homoerotic subtext was barely sub. Sure, Mikey and I were going to die laughing about it later, but right then I had to bite my tongue, and that was kind of painful.

I looked at him for a few moments, totally expressionless. Just long enough that he'd gone back to his homework. Just long enough to make him squirm. "What? You're creeping me out."

"I could've sworn I heard you say stop sleeping in your bed when you sneak out to see your girlfriend."

Mom and Dad never checked on me. Ever. I never gave them a reason to. Goff? Too many. Neither of us was stupid enough to think pillows under the blankets would fool them, but me in his bed? Physically we were nothing alike, but at least I made breathing sounds. We had a Jack and Jill bedroom setup where our rooms met in a common bathroom. We locked the bathroom door leading into the hallway and put the pillows in *my* bed, I moved to his, and he was out of there. He always showed his gratitude.

"You... That's harsh, man."

"Times are hard."

Goff threw down his pen. "Why're you doing this?"

"Because it's almost summer, which means fall's not that far away, which means neither is the prom, and it's never too early to present a united front."

"You're really twisted, you know that?"

I shrugged. "And you know she'll try to get you to take someone besides your girlfriend, since you quote, unquote haven't been dating that long."

"They're not that bad," Goff said, sighing.

"Have it your way, but don't come whining to me when Mom does exactly that." It's not that I was smarter than Goff. I wasn't. But I was smarter in different areas, like sneaking. It was like he didn't have an ounce of guile in him. Apparently, I received both our shares. Somehow, and despite getting him into endless trouble when we were children, he still trusted me. Maybe it's because as we grew older, I got him out of scrapes, at least when I knew about them in time.

Maybe I shouldn't have complained. Goff got the same kind of nonsense from our parents, too, and never mind that he had a girlfriend. She wasn't even a cheerleader. She was supersweet and amazingly intelligent. He met Laurel because I brought her home to study for AP Biology I. It took him a few months of whining like an Irish setter, but they eventually took to studying each other's biology. I knew this because Goff was too chickenshit to buy his own condoms, so I had to buy them for him.

Speaking of shit of whatever species, Goff was in it because a teammate was caught dealing molly. Goff's friend slash teammate was busted by the cops at a team party. Oddly enough what our parents freaked out about was that Geoff had alcohol on his breath. He blew a 0.12 as a matter of fact. I think that was half again the legal limit. Yeah, hi, Mom and Dad, he was at a party where the host was busted for dealing *Ecstasy*. You maybe want to focus on the larger picture? Or maybe they were, because I knew for a fact my brother didn't and wouldn't take drugs. Anyway, Goff couldn't fart without them breathing down his neck for a while.

But if I'd known about the party, I'd have told him to watch his step, because rumors of drug-dealing by members of the football team had been flying around school for weeks. At the very least, he might've limited himself to a beer or two instead of getting trashed. Then Goff could've told the olds, "Sorry, Mom and Dad, I know it showed bad judgment, but I planned to call Germy to come and get me." And I'd have absolutely covered for him. For that matter, he could have gotten trashed, and I'd still have picked him up if he had warned me in time to cover for him.

Weirdly enough, they were totally permissive where I was concerned. They thought I was a late bloomer and hoped the talks they gave Goff about sex applied to me, too, because they made me sit down and listen to every single one of them, not that they contained anything I needed to know. But the last one? I couldn't take it anymore and I cranked up the sarcasm. It bugged Dad, I knew that for sure, and I was pretty sure I managed to irritate Goff, and never mind the fact that he was sick of those talks too. Goff already knew not to get his girlfriend pregnant and to make sure *he* was in charge of *his* birth control.

Except for the condom buying. I was in charge of that.

"Could you maybe shut up, Germy? This is bad enough without your sniping."

Dad nodded. "Please listen to your brother. I get that you may be too old for these, but you're not making this easier on any of us. If you stop, I promise this will be the last one."

"You've said that every time, Dad. Yet here we are, another ho-hum day in paradise listening to these riveting talks," I said acidly. "I think we've got a lock on the prevention of premature grandparenthood. Not much else, but babies are definitely one sexually transmitted parasite we can rule out. Maybe someday we can move on to spirochetes."

"Jeremy..." Dad said in that warning tone of his. It held a hint of a threat, but what did I care? I'd heard it all my life and it had long since ceased to have the desired effect. It was more proof that I was the changeling, the odd Babcock out.

These things were so stupid. Take today's lecture. Please. Dad actually had the nerve to refer to the labia as a butterfly. How the hell was I supposed to keep a straight face when confronted with that? Dad was going on about female anatomy again, trying to help Goff—and presumably me—locate the G-spot. I would never need to know, and based on the noises issuing from Goff's room of an evening, he already knew exactly where to find it. What I needed—what we both needed—was basic information on sexually transmitted infections. Anatomy had been covered in eighth-grade sex ed.

Yet this was vintage Dad, blithely charging ahead, with Goff in tow more or less willingly and me digging in my heels every step of the way. I could not say Dad never heard, if only because sound waves did stimulate his auditory nerves. It never changed his behavior, however, and trying to persuade Dad was like arguing with the wind for all the good it did, at least not once he had a notion fixed in his mind. Mom had some facility in managing him, but then, she had more experience. Goff and I were only teenagers, so what did we know? I was convinced that was how Dad's thought processes ran. The bizarrissimo part of it all was that Goff was the good twin whereas I questioned everything, fighting anything I thought absurd with tooth and claw. I had even overheard Dad say as much when he thought he was unobserved. Yet Dad—both parents, really—kept Goff on a shorter leash.

I thought this different treatment was because of our different sports, I really did. Football? Sure. Everyone knew the deal or thought they did. What they really knew was the reputation that came from a bunch of idiotic movies. Goff sure wasn't like that, and most of his football friends weren't either. But crew? They had no idea about crew, not really, and never mind the stupid amounts of parental involvement my club required. No, when Mom and Dad were in college, rowers were pale, muscular gods and goddesses who walked the campuses, ate obscene amounts of food after their early-morning practices without gaining a pound, and stuck mainly with their own kind. They told me as much. That my club's juniors program practiced in the afternoon must have thrown them off my scent, because I had a tan despite the sunblock.

Seriously, I got away with murder. Or at least I did the summer before my senior year, and the person I killed—or almost killed—was myself. After that? I lived on Cellblock Q.

Chapter Two

Spring went in either direction in the Sacramento Valley, sometimes on a daily basis. One year we had to wear parkas into June because it kept raining, but other years the weather was a mixed bag with warm weather one week and thunderstorms the next. That year, lightning and hail added a certain zest to rowing. It definitely gave me an appreciation for what crews in the Midwest and Southeast routinely put up with. This year, we lucked out. Spring was springlike: cool in the morning but warming up nicely by lunch.

I sat outside at lunch with the rest of the rowing geeks, or at least those of us from Cap City's junior crew who did not assort themselves into some other clique. There weren't that many of us, and we fit on a couple of picnic tables under some trees on the quad. I never felt like I belonged anywhere else, so I sat with my crewmates by default. I lacked Goff's popularity. Seriously, my brother could go anywhere and be welcomed. He was a jock and top of the heap in that group, so yeah. He earned good marks, too, so other than the hardcore geeks and

LARPers who hated jocks as part of the order of things, he always had a table with the brainiacs. Sometimes they were not sure what to make of him, but his outgoing personality smoothed the way.

I wished I could be that kind of chameleon. The jocks could not figure me out, because crew did not fit into their canned hierarchy. Or maybe they just took their cues from some of the coaches who disliked the fact that there were jocks they did not control. I was just a rower; I did not want to get involved in the politics. I couldn't. As long as *my* coaches kept me from having to take any kind of mandatory PE, I was happy, and I got enough exercise at the boathouse, thanks all the same.

Because I displayed actual muscle development, the people in my AP and honors classes could not make heads or tails of me either. I took the same classes. We studied together sometimes. But other than Laurel and a few of her friends, I could not get the time of day from that crowd. Even then I had to be careful because if I spent too much time with Laurel, Goff would think I was putting the moves on her. It was another reason to come out to him. I thought some of the athletes from the more intellectual sports like cross-country or swimming might be able to deal, but no. It was me and the other rowers, even if the majority of them were JV. Most of the guys in my boat went to other schools, which sucked. I wished I could say I got tired of their mangy butts, but when I was on my own at school, I had to admit I missed them.

Or maybe that was just the nature of high school, and I was melodramatic. Or maybe I was socially awkward? Regardless, I hung there in the background like wallpaper, basically invisible unless I did something tacky, in which case *everyone* noticed me, but not in a good way.

I'd never admit this, but I kind of envied Mikey. For starters, he was a lot more social. Or maybe he was a lot more grounded? He knew who he was, never mind that he was only a sophomore. Some people were like that. I didn't begrudge him that, but I wished I could figure out who I was. I think Mikey sat with me so I did not sit by myself. He told me I was the only person he knew who could be so alone in a crowd. Or maybe he had a crush on me. It could've gone either way. The motives of sophomores were dreadfully obscure, so I was not inclined to argue.

As I listened to people chatter, I wished I could tell Goff about me. I was pretty sure he knew something was up. What was worse, it was starting to come between us. Goff sensed something. He had to, if only because I was out to my team and rowers gossiped like there was a prize for it. I knew I was the sensitive twin, but he was not stupid. The thought of telling him scared the crap out of me. My parents were worthless, so he was all I had. What if I told him and he freaked? Then I'd be alone. We had been there for each other since before we were born, and I couldn't face things without him. Couldn't face *life* without him, really. But if I didn't tell him, that might happen anyway.

"You're quiet," Mikey said.

Caught red-handed. "Just thinking."

He nudged my shoulder. "About?"

"My History Day project." Junior year in California meant US History, and since Davis was basically Lake Wobegon—all the children were above average—we had to participate in History Day. If we made an A on our projects, it went in the grade books as a double A, meaning we could skip a test—including the final—or replace a grade. Not bad.

Mikey made a face. "Is this what I have to look forward to?"

"Only if you take honors US History." I said that, but we both knew he probably would. People who didn't live here didn't really understand what it was like. Parents didn't apply academic pressure. They didn't have to. We internalized it and did it to ourselves.

"What's your topic again?"

"The Fourth Amendment's protections against unreasonable searches and seizures in the electronic age, specifically whether or not the police need warrants when it comes to using text messages as evidence in criminal proceedings. You see—"

"That's enough." Mikey held up a hand. His smile took the sting off it. "Anything about the NSA? That's topical and sounds like it relates."

I shuddered. "Oh God no. For one thing, the legal analysis is all over the place. For another, federal judges are issuing contradictory rulings. It's just not something I want to touch."

For a lie to avoid telling him what I was really thinking about, History Day wasn't bad. It helped that I actually had to work on it.

"I was going to ask if you wanted to hang out after practice this weekend…"

I thought as much. "We can always do homework. Your place or mine?"

"Let's play that by ear, 'kay?" Mikey said. "Whichever house is quieter."

I bumped his shoulder. "We need to go. Weight training, remember?"

"Like I could forget." Mikey rolled his eyes. "Tons of fun. Oh wait!" he said as I rose from the picnic table. "Are you driving today?"

"Yep. You need a ride?" We went through this ritual almost every day. I always drove to practice because the boathouse was in West Sacramento, about fifteen miles away. Goff and I shared a car, but his practice was at school, so I drove to practice and then drove back by school to pick him up. That had been one of the conditions of Mom and Dad buying us a car. If Goff had already gotten a ride home, he texted me. Mikey didn't live that far from us, and he always chipped in for gas.

"Yeah." Mikey sighed. "Until I get my own car… I'm sorry to keep mooching off you."

"You're not mooching, and besides, our coaches keep hassling us to carpool, right?" It was true, they were all over that, and besides, between Cap City, UC Davis, and CalPac, parking was at a premium. Cap City's junior crew was the low spot on the totem pole. The more people we crammed in our cars, the less we had to listen to Coach Lodestone bitch about it.

Mikey smiled shyly. "Great, I'll meet you by your car after seventh period."

"What about weights? I'll see you in about ten minutes."

"Then too." I could only smile and shake my head as he walked away.

*

The state required PE through the tenth grade, but rowing counted for independent study PE and got the junior varsity crews off the hook. After that, no one had to take PE, but I rowed so I might as well have gotten some credits for it. All any of us required was our coach's signature on some form for the athletic department and we were covered. Easy peasy, right?

Wrong. Some of the coaches of other teams resented the fact that we existed. That was the only reason I could think of for their opposition. Naturally, the coach who oversaw weight training for all the independent-study athletes was one of the noisiest in his opposition. I thought he should take it up with Coach Lodestone. Instead he made passive-aggressive comments during weight training.

Whatever. It was not like I was all that fond of weights. I only lifted to make the boats move faster. It was funny. I had a goal. I lifted for a reason. But every day I trudged to the locker room, quashing my fight-or-flight responses. It was not much of a mystery. It was the locker room. Actual hell for the high school closet case was any place with naked guys. I wanted to look. No, I had to look. I couldn't help it. It was a biological compulsion. I kept my head down, trained on my locker, my duffel bag, my feet, anything but the guys around me, all of them smokin' hot. I couldn't look, not openly. I was afraid, because if I looked, I'd react, and my own flesh would betray me. I knew there were other gay guys at school, if only because my best friend was dressing out the next row over. I'd even sensed other eyes on me when I dressed out for PE, but I could never look around, because if I did, I'd get hard at the wrong time and then someone would know.

I was out to the guys on the crew, so I wasn't a total closet case. Mikey certainly knew, but I didn't look at him. It would've been like looking at my brother. Kind of. Anyway, I didn't look at them, they didn't hassle me. We were all friends, and you don't perv on your friends. The moral economy of the boner and all that. Besides, our lockers were in different rows. As for the other guys who lifted this hour? I had excellent peripheral vision, and some of them had starred in my fantasies this whole school year. Living on the edge, you know?

"Hey, man."

I met Francisco's eyes on the way out of the locker room. "Hey."

"More hoops. Couldn't you just squeal?" Francisco was as enthusiastic about this as I was. Cisco was a good guy and one of the other varsity rowers at Davis High from my boat.

"If we pull anything this close to the Crew Classic, Lodestone will kill Robertson."

Coach Robertson, our babysitter for the next hour, wanted us to warm up by shooting hoops.

Cisco grinned. "From your lips to God's ears. I'm so ready for all this to be over."

"No kidding." And I wasn't. Overtraining was no joke. After the Crew Classic, I was either going to sleep for a month, get sick, or both.

With that cheerful thought, we put minimal effort into the warm-up. We both knew there was a better way to warm up, and it was called an ergometer, the specialized rowing machine that dominated our sport, and we accepted no substitutes. Also, that would've been functional training for us, and I wasn't exaggerating. The Crew Classic was in two weeks, and all the rowers were hovering on the edge of overtraining. Lodestone knew it was a fine line, and he was being ultracareful. The question was, was Robertson?

After that warm-up, we shuffled into the weight room to do our thing. The cool thing about this section was not only that it was full of rowers, but it was full of *all* the rowers, both boys' and girls' junior crews. A lot of the men's crews looked upon the women's crews as prime dating material, and I didn't blame them. I'd noticed that rowers stuck to our own kind when dating. Who else understood the demands on our time? "I can't, I have crew" didn't sound like an excuse or a cop-out when you said it to another rower. Me, I regarded the presence of the women as the social hour. I didn't think my teammates realized how many of the ladies liked the other ladies. Oh well, they'd figure it out. Maybe.

At least resistance training was somewhat mindless, so long as we watched our form. At this point, I and my fellow rowers were using weight machines rather than free weights because the machines made it a little easier to let go. Machines may not have provided as good a workout as free weights, but this close to the biggest spring race, we were as strong as we were going to be. We weren't trying to build, just trying to maintain and avoid injury.

As soon as I could during weights, I got in my zone. Coach Robertson hated iPods in the weight room but was too lazy to do anything about them. I could appreciate sloth when it worked for me. Since I loathed the death metal the meatheads listened to, I dialed up a dance or alt-rock playlist and tuned out. Abject misery wasn't anything I needed to share with anyone, not even my teammates. I could always pull an earbud out if it was time to visit. People assumed I wasn't paying much attention if I had my earbuds in, simply because they weren't. That often worked to my advantage.

Once in a while, I watched Mikey lift. You could tell from looking at people and the mistakes they made who'd make varsity soon and who never had a chance. He was a sophomore, and it was the end of the school year. Physically he might not have looked like much yet, but he was an ape on the ergs, pulling with a strength disproportionate to his size. Seriously, some of the guys in the varsity boats needed to be scared for their seats. They weren't, but they should be. He was an erg ninja, all stealthy and smooth, whispering in for the kill. I couldn't figure out why nobody had noticed him yet. I was fast, faster than he'd be for a while, but I had a feeling it was a good thing next year was my senior year. As soon as Mikey's stroke in the boat matched his up-and-coming erg scores? He'd row varsity.

Sometimes, however, I felt eyes on me, and when I did, they usually belonged to Mikey. Yeah, he liked to stare at me. On the one hand, it was kind of cool. The guy seemed like he was into me. Ego candy always tasted good. On the other hand, could he not look away once in a while? Maybe in the showers? I think I would have liked it better if I knew the candy didn't want to eat me back. It wasn't like I was going to say anything. I might have imagined it, and when you were a closeted gay guy in high school and your best friend was another gay guy, you kind of let things slide.

I used the leg press to practice starts at the beginning of the stroke: explode off the foot boards for a hard start. Bend those oars, dammit. My quads were ripped, nice to look at, I guess, but getting them to that point had been brutal.

"Get off that."

I looked up to see one of the meatheads from one of the sportball teams. Goff would have known which one. "Go away, Stephens. I'm using it."

"I want to use it." Stephens actually looked confused, like no one had told him no before, which I knew for a fact wasn't true. Word got around school, after all.

I nodded toward the dry-erase board behind me with my chin. "Get in line."

"Do back squats. They'll give you a nice ass. Whoever's fucking it will appreciate the effort, fag."

Ever been in a room when all conversation stopped? I'd thought it was just a figure of speech. I stared up at him. The only noise in the room was the swamp cooler and a radio playing in the background. I felt rowers around me, my tribe.

"That's pretty big talk for someone who can't figure out how to use a rubber. Do you need lessons?"

Probably not the best thing to have said to someone when I was basically trapped in a weight machine, but he had a lot of hostile witnesses. Stephens glared at me.

"Is there a problem?" Coach Robertson said, finally taking an interest in the fact that one of his jocks had made a feeble attempt at homophobic bullying.

"No, Coach," Stephens grunted.

"Too bad you didn't have the kind of aim you gave Missy during that last game before the play-offs. You might not have bungled the shot at the championships," I stage-whispered as I pulled myself up and out of the leg press.

Coach Robertson whipped his head around to glare at me while Stephens turned beet red, but there wasn't anything either could do to me because nothing I'd said was untrue. Stephens *had* bungled that shot, he *had* cost the team a shot at the state championships, and he *had* knocked up his girlfriend.

"If you were on my team, I'd never let you get away with that. Your coach will hear about this," Coach Robertson said.

"Will Vice Principal Gutslinger hear about Stephens's homophobic comments and your lack of reaction?" Cisco said.

"Class dismissed," Coach Robertson growled, waving us all out.

We all headed back to the locker rooms before the bell rang. I lacked the energy to care. It wasn't like this was the first time I'd heard crap like that or the first time the teachers hadn't done anything about it.

I didn't have a lot of time to shower off, but I managed to dawdle. I didn't dare risk wood. This was turning me into a nutcase. What was I saying? It already had. It was the same thing every day. First, changing and being afraid of my body's betrayal. Then weights, and finally the terror of the shower. Why couldn't I do this? They all knew I was gay and were okay with it, or most of them. So why couldn't I shower? Or maybe they only tolerated me because I didn't shower at the same time? I locked my throat so I didn't scream, but I wanted to and one of these days I would. I banged my head on my locker door instead. Yesterday I had pretended I had to go to the bathroom to kill time. My teacher for my next class had threatened to call my parents—again—if I was tardy too many more times.

By the time I got into the showers, Mikey was there waiting. He wasn't obvious or anything, but I doubted it was a coincidence. Once or twice might've been, but almost every day strained that to the breaking point. I seriously could not imagine what he saw in me.

"Dude... Remy, it's okay. It really is," Mikey said softly.

All I could do was stare at his face. I shook my head slowly, unable to speak. Mikey looked at me sadly as I washed myself as fast as I could without looking down.

But if I didn't look down, I thought as I ran to sixth period, how do I know how big he is?

Chapter Three

So that was my life—school, crew, and casual homophobia in the People's Republic of Davis. None of this addressed my present predicament. I was almost done with my junior year of high school, and I still had this tiresome condition: still a virgin, no boyfriend, and no hope of landing one. I didn't have any proof, but I had the strangest feeling that Mikey would be more than ready to step up, but that was...weird, like my younger brother or something. If said younger brother was getting cruisy. Also, I knew I needed him as a friend, and a friend he'd stay for as long as my left hand worked. Besides, if he became my boyfriend, then people would've known I leaned that way, too, no matter how on the down low we kept things. I wasn't ready for that.

And yet... Sure, I made noises about keeping him as a friend and thinking of him in a fraternal sort of way, but I was drawn to Mikey so strongly. I mean, how could I not have been? I was incredibly lonely when it came down to it, and he was the only other person I knew for sure was gay. I mean, he was in the Gay Straight Alliance, and since he wasn't straight... Then there was my undeniable attraction to him. Were I to be honest with myself, it didn't matter to me that I was a year older or he a year younger. It was like he had a hook in my nose. He could've led me anywhere. I guess it was a good thing he was such a (ahem) straight arrow. I drove myself a little crazier every day with this.

Thank God I had rowing or I would've been a total mess. No matter what else happened in my day, I always counted on the ritual of crew, starting with meeting Mikey at my car. Davis High had an open campus, meaning we could leave school whenever we weren't supposed to be in class. Lunch in town? Sure. Drive yourself to a doctor's appointment? Not a problem. Every so often some group of parents launched a campaign to close the campus, but a bit of digging revealed their kids were the ones abusing the privilege and bringing themselves to the attention of the police. Nice try, assholes, but don't punish the rest of us because you failed Parenting 101.

Anyway, crew. I knew we were going to be worked like the dogs we were, and I never cared. That was not quite true. I cared a lot, because I looked forward to it, even needed it. In some ways the boathouse was home. I knew everyone and everyone knew me. We all contributed to something greater than the parts of the whole.

I always felt the annoyances of the day melt as we hit the road for the boathouse. It was the beginning of the ritual. Some of us changed at school, but most changed at the boathouse. The women always took the singles house, the boathouse that held the single-person boats; the men the fours house, the boathouse that held the four-seaters of various configurations.

Mikey and I changed near each other. Cisco wasn't too far away. Unlike the locker room at school, it did not matter because we had all known each other for so long. Even the new guys were absorbed quickly. I think one of the recent additions looked at me changing just after school started and said, "You're gay?" like he had a problem with it. I stood up as I was pulling on my Lycra shorts and said, "Yeah, so what?" The fact that I was taller, more muscular, and filled out my shorts better shut him down pretty quickly.

It was the ritual.

Then we took oars to the dock and started to warm up while we waited for our coaches, at least those of us who were smart did, usually with a light jog or on the rowing machines. After group exercises and warm-ups, our coaches posted the boatings. Even within the varsity squads, where a rower sat in a boat changed from practice to practice as, like in my case, Coach Lodestone moved his rowers about to see who rowed better where and which combinations of men moved boats faster. Lodestone only stopped moving us right before races, and even then, he still sometimes made last-minute tweaks to lineups.

The ritual.

I came alive at the boathouse. I had given up trying to help other people understand, although my dad claimed he saw a faraway look in my eyes when I talked about rowing. I knew that had been why he'd gone to bat for me when Mom had threatened to make me quit when I'd had some trouble with my grades in the ninth grade.

"Dina, I've never seen him passionate about anything. He's passionate about this."

"But—"

"Not this time. We'll hire a tutor."

I'd learned to manage my time better, and it all sorted itself out, more or less. That was the first time I recalled Dad going to bat for me. Actually, it was the last time I remembered Dad going to bat for me. I tried to remember that when Dad worked my nerves, as during those birth-control lectures. That made it easier to remember.

Sometimes people asked me why I did it, why I put up with the demands on my time, and in all honesty, crew devoured all that free time, burped in my face, and then demanded more. I never got enough sleep, and yes, my grades suffered, even though I had dragged them back up to acceptable levels and qualified for the AP/honors track. I had no real social life and no outside interests beyond crew and whatever else I had to do to appear well-rounded on college-entrance essays.

I've talked to masters rowers, the adult members of Cap City Rowing. They took the morning shift at the boathouse. Some of them get the same distant look in their eyes talking about the sun rising on the water, the same look Dad thought he saw in my eyes when I spoke of the sun setting over those same waters. I wish I knew how to tell people that's why I did it, that's why I sacrificed everything. That was why we all did it. We bent our backs, we ripped the skin of our hands to shreds on the oar handles, we worked our muscles until we felt nothing but the blunt pain of lactic acid, we forced our heart rates up beyond our aerobic thresholds until we felt that sharp stab in our lungs only to let our pulses fall to do it again and again and again, we pushed ourselves beyond exhaustion, all in the hope that when we did it tomorrow, it might be a little easier. Because when the cox'n cried "Way 'nough!" and we gunwaled our oars and let the boat run beneath us as we looked up into the setting sun, our senses dulled with fatigue, we knew we had done our best and the sun had blessed us. Only then did we feel satisfaction.

That was why I rowed.

Only other rowers understood that.

That was the ritual of crew.

After one such practice, when I was still flying from the high I got from a perfect row, I conceived the idea that helped me solve the problem of my annoying V-card.

The Crew Classic was the next weekend, but the boats left the next day. The trailer carrying them couldn't exactly drive fast, and San Diego was a long way south as it was. With the Grapevine and the pass through the Tehachapis to contend with, the truck pulling the boat trailer could only drive slow and steady.

Cap City operated under the assumption that if we rowed it, we rigged it, or de-rigged it, as the case was that afternoon. Fortunately, with both the gentlemen's and ladies' squads, as varsity men and women were called, the de-rigging went fairly quickly. Since both Coach Lodestone and Sabrina Littlewolf—the ladies' coach—planned to row a mixed double just for fun while they were down there, I was de-rigging a boat for them. The perks of being a varsity rower and the coach's pet, I guess.

The boathouse yard was controlled pandemonium—if that wasn't an oxymoron—and so the stranger's presence wasn't really an issue. No one on the junior crew knew all the masters rowers anyway, so what was one more person wandering around? That no one paid him the slightest heed probably irritated him, but no one else thought anything of it. We were busy.

Soon enough, Stranger Guy showed up in my peripheral vision, a faculty highly developed from not looking at people in locker rooms. For one thing he was hot. College age, if I had to guess, and definitely fit. The tight polo shirt he wore left little to the imagination, not that that stopped me. I already imagined a lot. He looked like he was making his way toward me. I was working by myself, and I wasn't rushing back and forth under the command of a cox'n.

I didn't want to look like I'd been watching him, because that would give the game away, but it's not like I'd been all that effective with the wrench I was allegedly employing to loosen the bolts on the riggers of the double either. How many times did the wrench have to slip off the bolt before I could say I was officially paying no attention at all to the de-rigging?

"Uh...excuse me?"

I pretended to be concentrating on the task at hand, but I felt his eyes on me. "Oh, hey."

"Is this the Capital City Rowing Club's boathouse?" Stranger Guy was a little shorter than me, but a lot more built, more like a lacrosse player or a wrestler than a rower. He also had the bluest eyes I'd ever seen, the kind that made you think someone wore tinted contacts, but no, they looked like his real eyes.

I shook my head. I was so glad I had a boat between us because parts of me were sitting up and begging. "Yeah." My voice cracked. I coughed. "Yes, it is. Can I help you with something?"

"I'm looking for the Adaptive Rowing program. Do you know anything about it?" He smiled, like he'd noticed me noticing him.

"Adaptive rowing... I'm not sure if either of the coaches are here yet, but you'll want to talk to either Nick Bedford—I think he's still in charge of it—or Brad Sundstrom." I absolutely could not breathe around either man, and the cool thing was that both men were gay, so neither could bust me for it because the chances were high both had been there themselves. Not that I appeared on their radar, and even if I had, I'd never have done anything. They wouldn't have either. They were both married, and I respected that. Their husbands or partners or whatever term they preferred were super nice guys too. I wanted that for myself; I didn't want to break up someone else's. No, all I could do around them was stare discreetly and hope they never caught me.

Stranger Guy kind of rolled his eyes at me, like I hadn't answered his question, and maybe I hadn't. I didn't know. I found it hard to think when I looked at him. "Okay, next question. Where do I find those guys? If they're here, that is."

Guess I hadn't answered his question. I felt myself turning red. Maybe he'd think it was a sunburn? "Oh, sorry! The adaptive rowing program is housed in the singles house. It's on the other side of this building. Just follow this sidewalk," I said, pointing, "turn left at the corner and keep going. Just a couple of things. If you're not used to boathouses, boats have the right of way and 'heads up!' means duck because you're about to be hit with a boat."

"Heads up. Got it," Stranger Guy said. "What's the other one?"

"The women's teams change in the singles house, so if the door's even partially closed, make a lot of noise and knock before entering." By the end of a given year, the boundaries of who changed where got a little casual, particularly at regattas. The thrill had worn off, let's just put it that way. With the Crew Classic coming up, we'd be changing behind vans or holding towels up for each other, eyes averted. But Stranger Guy? He'd better not peek.

"Thanks for the warning," he said. "I'll go see what I can find, and thanks."

He smiled at me, and I swear my knees weakened. "No problem."

I got back to work, or at least tried. I had lost a certain amount of manual dexterity after talking to

Stranger Guy. I finally set the wrench down and stilled my hands. I took a deep breath and exhaled, trying to regain my composure. I looked up to see Stranger Guy leaning against the boathouse watching me, a half smile on his face, one eyebrow raised. He wasn't just watching me, he was eye-fucking me. I knew the signs because I'd done it enough myself.

Then I realized why. After practice, I'd pulled the top of my unisuit down to cool off. Stranger Guy stared right at my chest, pecs, abs, and light dusting of hair. Like I always did, I flushed red from my forehead all the way down my chest. I felt it all heat up. I might as well have been standing there in my underwear. Boxer briefs might actually have covered more, come to think of it. There would be no hoping my blush would be mistaken for a sunburn, not this time.

I swore Stranger Guy laughed as he turned around and went about his business. *Screw you, too, buddy.* The humiliation was enough to break whatever spell Stranger Guy and lust had put me under. I yanked the straps of my uni up and got back to work, anger steadying my hand as I loosened the bolts. But who was I angrier at, Stranger Guy or myself? After all, he'd just walked up and looked me up and down. I was the one who'd started panting. Was this the kind of thing that got easier when you grew up? I sure hoped so because this was torment, pure and simple, and the tormentor was me.

I had finished de-rigging the double. I'd wrapped the riggers with bungee cords so they'd stay together in the bottom of the boat trailer on the trip to San Diego. I had already placed the bolts and their washers and nuts back on the boat, just where they were supposed to go. It probably didn't make a whole lot of difference. If a bolt got lost, it'd just be replaced, but I did what I'd been trained to, and that was carefully match nuts to the bolts I'd taken them off. But I had to tighten them down. Too loose and the vibrations of the truck would cause them to fall off during the drive, resulting in one or both coaches fussing at me. Too tight, and—

"You know, pulling the top up just makes it hotter."

I jumped, startled like a cat. "Jeez!"

Stranger Guy took a step back but looked no less amused. "Sorry, didn't mean to scare you like that."

He looked anything but sorry. He had that same half smile and some kind of look in his eye that could've had me naked in minutes if I weren't so terrified. "Thanks for the directions. I found what I...wanted. My name's Josh."

Suddenly I had the feeling he wasn't talking about adaptive rowing anymore. My breath caught in my chest, like my ribs had turned into steel bands and I couldn't get any air.

"I'm—" I coughed. "—um, Remy."

"Well, Um Remy, it's great to meet you. Hopefully, I'll see you around."

Stranger Guy—Josh—walked backward for a few moments to maintain eye contact, smirking. All I could do was stare. I was pretty sure my mouth hung open.

Then Josh turned around, and I snapped out of it. What had just happened? The wood in my uni knew what had happened. So why couldn't I believe it? I glanced down at the double I had just de-rigged and spotted a small piece of paper that hadn't been there before.

I stared at it for what felt like forever, hardly daring to breathe, my pulse roaring in my ears.

I snatched it up before anyone else saw it. Was it...? It was. A scrap of paper with a telephone number, just a number, no name. Davis, judging by the area code, and I doubted I'd ever forget his name anyway.

I should've thrown it away. I was terrified. However grown-up I felt, however ready I thought I was for this, reality hit me. I was a juvenile, a high schooler, contemplating an adult's game, and there was no way I was prepared for something like this. If I'd been asked earlier that afternoon, I'd have said yes. Right then? I think I could've thrown up. I wanted to blow chunks right there in the boatyard. I also wanted to run home and hide. But I couldn't, could I?

I was just a kid, but the thing was, Goff and I were first asked what our majors were when we were fourteen. Weird, right? Even though we were not identical, we'd had that in common from an early age. We had used it to our advantage too. Earlier this year, we'd gotten fake IDs, although neither of us had had the balls to use them for anything. I think Geoff had toyed with the idea of buying beer for football parties but wasn't sure it was worth the hassle if he got caught. After that party with the molly bust, I couldn't blame him. Me, I'd always contemplated going to a gay club, but after my encounter at the boathouse with Josh, I threw that idea out. My reaction told me that was the last thing I was ready for, at least right then. A gay club? Jeez. I'd be terrified.

But I'd always looked old for my age, and now that I was about done with my junior year? I probably could've passed for a college student, and maybe not just a freshman. At least, that's what I hoped. Either that, or Josh was a pervert preying on underage guys, and maybe Coach Bedford or Coach Sundstrom needed to be told ASAP. I had no way of knowing.

"Hey, Remy! You about done?" Mikey said, walking up.

I'd never been more grateful to see him in my life. I shoved the slip of paper in my uni. "You bet. As soon as we get the word, we're out of here."

*

As unnerved as I was, it's not like I dropped the pedal and drove home at ninety miles per hour to take a Silkwood shower. If nothing else, congested traffic at that time of day on the causeway connecting West Sacramento to Davis meant I was lucky to go fifty. That wasn't to say I didn't feel that scrap of paper burning against my skin as I drove, or that I didn't play Depeche Mode's "Strangelove" on a loop most of the way back to Davis.

I guess I was lucky everyone in the car knew my hang-up with '80s music, because no one threatened me with grievous bodily harm. Either that, or we'd been worked hard enough that no one had the energy to protest. My mind raced in overdrive as I kept coming back to the words "I'm always willing to learn/When you've got something to teach," only it was Josh I heard saying, "I'll make it all worthwhile."

As we pulled into Davis High's parking lot, Mikey made a face and grabbed for my iPhone. He switched it from "repeat" and changed the song. "That's enough of *that*."

I swapped out the two rowers I'd given a ride to for my brother. Goff waved his hand in front of his face. "Whoa, Eau de Sweaty Rower."

Mikey rolled his eyes but let me field that one. "Good thing football players never sweat or roll around like dogs on the lawn."

"Yes, but a water sport. Can't you guys rinse off when you're done? Maybe jump in the river?" Goff rubbed his eyes. "Seriously, I'm tearing up."

"Dude, if you'd ever come out to the boathouse, you'd never, ever say that," Mikey said.

"He's not kidding. Our coaches had the water tested. They refused to tell us the results, but the waiver our parents signed was longer the next year." Honestly, Goff played a sport that put him at risk for traumatic brain injuries, so he lacked all ground to stand on. Where did he get this stuff? Oh, wait...

We dropped Mikey off, and Goff and I drove home.

"Good practice?" I said, meeting his eyes in the rearview mirror.

He roused himself enough to reply. "Yeah. You?"

"Short and hard, then de-rigging."

He groaned. "That's right, you leave day after tomorrow. Loser."

"Shut it. You'll have the bathroom to yourself."

I parked the car in front of the house. We grabbed our gear and trudged inside. A quick round of rock-paper-scissors-lizard-Spock determined that Goff would be showering first. I flopped onto my bed, not caring about dried sweat or anything else. I'd trudge downstairs after my shower and shovel food into my face to fuel my homework hours, but right then I needed to think. I pulled Josh's number out and stared at his blocky, masculine handwriting. I did not know what I expected, to be honest. Numbers that burned themselves into my retinas before the paper consumed itself in a puff of flame? Numbers that twisted and turned before my eyes, resolving into a message that told me to abandon all such notions lest I get myself into trouble? It was just a plain scrap of paper, but it held my attention in a way few other things had.

My reactions were all over the place and not even consistent. In one way, it turned me on. It represented physical evidence that some guy was hot for me. The sight of me half-dressed had revved someone up enough to make him do something about it. The sight of me fully dressed in my uni made it more intense for him. That feeling went right to my gut, curling around my spine and groin and warming me in a way I'd never felt before. It felt...powerful. Sexy. Like maybe this gay thing could work out after all, like maybe it wasn't just going to be me and my hand for the rest of my life. Because even if nothing happened with Josh, the very fact that he'd slipped me his number now meant someone else later on might find me worth his time, too, even if I did not understand why. I was just Remy, after all.

But that slip of paper with Josh's number scared me, too, and I knew I should've thrown it away before I'd left the boathouse. I hadn't even turned seventeen yet and wouldn't for another two months or so. When he'd asked me my name, I should have said, "Jailbait," and called him out as a fucking pervert. Hello? Look around, Josh. Notice how the boathouse is crawling with what are obviously teenagers? Just because I looked like I might've been an assistant coach didn't mean I was. But I always thought of the perfect thing to say...later. Even if on some level I needed to keep it, by keeping it I was playing that grown-up game. Sometimes acting older than my years could be good, but sometimes it could be scary, and right then it frightened me as much as it drew me in. The Voice of the Beehive had been so, so right, and oh how I wanted those scary kisses.

Finally, those numbers were seemingly my only link to an actual gay adult. In a weird way, that paper represented a lifeline to a world I knew would one day be mine, and when someone tosses you a life preserver, you don't throw it away.

Chapter Four

I couldn't say the timing of the Crew Classic was great. Finals and AP tests weren't too far in the future, but between the trip down and back, I'd be missing only one day of school—leaving hours before dawn on Friday morning on charter buses rented by Cap City, we re-rigged and practiced late Friday afternoon, raced all weekend, de-rigged on Sunday afternoon, and then drove north on Sunday night. We studied when we could on the drive and in between racing and spectating, because there was no way on earth we weren't cheering each other on. I mean, come on, we were a team.

I also could not say what made this particular regatta a "classic." There had only been forty or so. Forty. My parents had furniture older than that, only those were called antiques. Some of my friends lived in houses older than that. Did that make those homes "classics"? There were cars on the road older than that. That didn't make them classics, it made them rolling slag heaps that had been grandfathered into passing California's stringent air-pollution laws. I thought about things like that on the trip south when I wasn't studying, eating artificially flavored and colored crap, or just generally being a teenager.

Sure, the club dues were expensive, but they paid for things like this. Of course, there were the parent chaperones to contend with, and they watched us like hawks. I was secretly proud of the fact that the junior crew kept its collective nose clean. The big scandal a few years ago was that some of the rowers had TPed and egged someone's house. Sure, it had been a huge mess to clean up, but considering what other kinds of trouble teenagers could be getting into—drugs, alcohol, unplanned pregnancies—toilet-paper omelets looked great in comparison. Our coaches kept us pretty busy, and between fatigue and our grade requirements, we didn't have the time or the energy to get into real trouble. So, we rode in chartered buses, pretended to do our homework, and ate gross food under the very watchful eyes of chaperones. The boys' and girls' teams weren't even staying near each other. They weren't taking chances, our coaches and parents.

I sat next to Mikey. I contemplated telling him about Josh but didn't. Once I woke up for the day, I meant. Too many people around. Just because we all had headphones on or earbuds in didn't mean we were listening to music.

Somewhere south of Bakersfield, I'd had enough. I belched loudly and flopped over in my seat, right across whatever he was reading.

"That's disgusting."

I grinned up at him. "So?"

He considered me. "Is there something you want?"

"I'm bored. Entertain me."

It was automatic on his part, I was sure, but Mikey put one arm on my chest like it was no big deal. I tensed a little but didn't say anything. Instead I analyzed how I felt. It wasn't that bad. It felt...nice, actually. Once I got over my freak-out, I kind of relaxed into it.

"Entertain you?" Mikey started brushing my bangs off my forehead. "How am I supposed to do that?"

"I don't know," I said happily. "I'm sure you'll think of something. You're Mikey."

"You could always call me Mike, you know."

I looked up at him. Where'd that come from? "I could..." I drew the word out.

"Or you could keep on being the same annoying Germy we all know and loathe." Mikey sighed. He looked so serious as he looked down into my eyes, like there was something he wanted—no, needed—to tell me but couldn't right then. I couldn't discern what was on his mind, which confused me. Usually I knew what he was thinking, or could at least guess, but not this time. His hazel eyes held something different, something new. I noticed hidden depths there I had never seen before. I had no names for the things I saw, but I knew they were important, or would be some day. All I could do was stare back, although it made me increasingly uncomfortable, like he saw into my soul to the real me.

I noticed other things. His fingers were carding through my hair, his arm still on my chest, and I liked it. I reached up to touch his face—

"All right, you two lovebirds, break it up," someone called as he shuffled by, and the mood was broken.

Mikey and I blinked. I sat up in a hurry. The bus had stopped at some truck stop on the 5 in the middle of nowhere. Mikey stood and joined the line of people walking off the bus. He didn't look back, leaving me to wonder what had just happened, and more than that, what it meant.

*

I wish I could say I wouldn't spend the rest of the weekend obsessing over our weird exchange, but I knew that's exactly what I'd do, at least during idle moments. Thankfully, there weren't too many of those, but really, I had to wonder what was going on. Was I leaking pheromones or something? Because until this past week, people had proven pretty resistant to my so-called charms. When I looked in the mirror, I still saw plain ol' Remy. Whatever, I was just grateful I had a major regatta to distract me, because if nothing else, I would be too exhausted to spin my wheels over it. Or so I hoped.

Speaking of wheels, the bus pulled into the race venue midafternoon on Friday, or at least as close as it could get, before heading out for the houses where the boys' and girls' teams would be staying, where parent chaperones/volunteers would unload our gear for us and leave it in a huge heap for us to sort out. They were fantastic, but they couldn't be expected to do everything, right? All we kept was our backpacks, plus some workout clothes. We still had plenty of time to fit in a practice row, or go for a run, or check out the race venue. I planned to do all three.

For such a major regatta, the venue itself didn't occupy a lot of real estate, just a few blocks along Crown Point Shores on Mission Bay. The view of the bay was incredible, and the houses overlooking it? I bet they cost millions, but for that weekend I almost wished I lived up there. At the very least, I'd get a bird's-eye view of the entire venue, like the judges' stand and VIP enclosure at the halfway mark right on the beach and the jumbotrons bracketing them on either end for the less exalted spectators seated in the grass. Across the main walkway from the judges' stand and VIP pen were the vendors and food booths. Sometimes during the weekend, I'd hit the official T-shirt stand. I always bought one for Goff (he always got a baseball cap too), and this year I planned to buy a shirt for Laurel. Goff might've been my primary antagonist, but he was also my brother, and we were closer to each other than anyone else, and Laurel was such a sweetheart. Oh yeah, and Mom and Dad. They footed the bill for this adventure, after all, and they needed something to show for having one of their spawn in crew.

I had another reason for checking out the venue. I'd developed this weird ritual over the years. One of the first things I did at any regatta was walk as much of the course as I could. It wasn't too long before I heard footsteps behind me.

"Wait up, Remy."

I glanced over my shoulder and there was Cisco. Most of our boat trailed along behind him, along with a few of the junior varsity, the smarter ones. That included Mikey. "You walking the course?" Cisco said.

"I'm out here, aren't I?" Seriously, don't ask stupid questions.

Cisco flicked one of my ears. "Don't be an ass."

"Ow!" I rubbed the shell of my ear. "That goes for you too."

"So, what do you think?" Cisco asked me as we gazed out at the course.

I snorted. "What do I think? I think it looks great...right now."

And it did. The weather was gorgeous. With any luck, it would hold, but on the coast the weather could change with minimal provocation. I'd seen it turn nasty in the middle of a race weekend, and this was only my third Crew Classic. So had the Cap City coaches, according to the stories they told. All the rowers had had to sit through those stories enough times that we could sing along as our coaches recited them.

I looked at Cisco and the rest of our boat slyly. "Know what else I think? I think we need to get the JVs up here and make *them* identify what'll turn rough if the weather goes to hell."

Jack, our three seat, grinned. "Excellent idea." He turned to the junior varsity rowers. "Front and center, children!"

They looked at each other nervously. As a rule, Cap City's junior crew didn't haze, but I guess they thought there was a first time for everything.

"Now, now, none of that," I said. "We're walking the course to see what could potentially bite us in the ass during the race, especially if the weather turns feral."

"But you guys have all been here before," one of them said.

Cisco nodded. "Yes, we have, but every year's different."

"And if the weather turns, it won't matter whether we have any experience here or not; it'll be entirely new and definitely unfriendly," I said. "So, c'mon. All the way to the start line, or as close as we can get. You'll see what I mean. Pay attention to the course. See if you can spot any potential problems."

"Knowledge is power. Seriously, if you're prepared for potential problems, you won't be spooked when your cox'n calls them out," Jack said.

Mikey nodded. I think he was as close to a team captain as the JV had. "It can't hurt. Let's humor them."

"So, what do you see?" Cisco said.

"The sidewalk ends," one of the JVs said. "This is as far as we can go."

As far as observations went, this was along the lines of noticing an aircraft carrier bearing down on you. The sidewalk gave out around the five-hundred-meter mark. If we kept walking, we'd get wet.

"So. This is where the sidewalk ends. There's a bit of a breeze, but it's a gorgeous afternoon, right?" I nodded encouragingly. "So, take a look out there. Tell me how big you think those swells are."

We all looked out to the bay, or to the sheltered part of it that we could see, that part we'd be racing on tomorrow. Our backs were to the bridge over the bay.

"One foot, maybe?" Mikey said.

Cisco shrugged. "That's as good a guess as any. I wouldn't be comfortable sculling out there, not even in an open-water craft."

I turned around and pointed to the bridge. "We were looking at sheltered water. Over there is the rest of the bay and eventually the ocean. So, what happens if the wind comes up? What kind of chop do you think we're going to get at the five-hundred-meter mark? What kind of crosswind?"

"Point made," Mikey said. The rest of his squad nodded.

"This is why I walk the course, or at least what of it I can get to," I said, "even on a course I'm familiar with. Or take a course like Lake Natoma. It's in our backyard, relatively speaking, but the conditions change depending on what the runoff from the Sierra Nevadas is or what the dam operators have been doing to the water levels. It changes within a season."

So, we walked back to where we expected our boat trailer to park, trying to spot potential problems to set the less experienced rowers' minds at ease with possible solutions to different contingencies. We couldn't predict everything, but that wasn't the point, not for my race-course walks and not for taking the JVs with us. I did it as part of my race preparations, and Cisco wanted to include the junior varsity to allay their anxieties.

Cisco caught up to me afterward. "Let's see if the novice coaches cotton on to this."

"I wonder if Lodestone or Littlewolf have mentioned anything about this to them?" I said. "I guess that'd be a way to find out if they think it's of any value."

"Even if they don't, we get value out of it, and that's all that matters." Cisco paused. I could tell he was building up to something. "So...what's up with you and Mikey?"

I thought about that for a moment. "I have absolutely no idea."

"So, the bus..."

"Your guess is as good as mine." Interesting that people—okay, one person—were asking me about it already. We hadn't even been off the bus more than a couple of hours.

Fortunately, the trailer and re-rigging awaited us all. Normally re-rigging's a chore, but at that moment? Never happier to get my chores done.

*

After the gentlemen's crew fit an hour or so of light rowing in, we made it back to our temporary accommodations. The team had rented what looked like mansions, and I assumed the girls' teams found themselves in similar accommodations somewhere in the vicinity of Mission Bay. I hadn't had time to text my friends on the ladies' crew yet. Anyway, we stayed in huge places, eight or ten rooms at least, plus a lot of floor space. I was sure the neighbors loved the buses showing up, but at least they didn't stick around long after dropping us off.

Our gear was in an enormous heap, but the other squads had saved us some room. Or maybe it was the coaches and chaperones. Whatever. I was too tired and hungry to care at that point.

Food me, already.

Team dinners... I hated to say it, especially given how much I loved my team, but I hated team dinners. I've heard some stupid saying about a committee being a creature with forty-eight legs—three varsity boats, eight rowers each, two legs apiece—and no head. That pretty much summed up team dinners. With food allergies, dietary preferences, and people acting like princesses thrown in, we were lucky we managed to eat at all. It was not like I believed in very much at all or for very long, but all I could say was thank God or whomever for the parent volunteers who cooked all the nights we were down there. They spared us all of that. Not only was cooking in cheaper than eating out—and this sport was freakin' expensive enough as it was—but it tasted better. So that first night down there, they fed us pasta, lots and lots of pasta.

After dinner, the varsity rowers cycled through the showers to clean the bay off us. Saltwater didn't feel all that good when it dried. Most of us headed to bed after that. Most of us. I waited until things were quiet and then texted Mikey.

REMY: *You awake?*

He must've been because he replied almost immediately.

MICHAEL: *Yep.*

REMY: *Feel like talking?*

MICHAEL: *Meet U upstairs on the roof.*

REMY: *???*

MICHAEL: *There's a patio up there.*

REMY: *OK*

Five minutes later, there we were, both dressed in sweats to ward off the evening chill. Mikey's devoured him, making him look somehow vulnerable.

"Hi," Mikey said softly.

I had a feeling it wasn't because we were trying not to get caught by our chaperones.

"Hi." I waved diffidently. I carefully lifted a deck chair and set it next to his. "So..."

"So?"

I sighed. "Are we okay?"

"What do you mean?"

No, that wasn't evasive or anything. "I feel like we've been avoiding each other since the bus."

Mikey sighed. "I don't get you."

"Cut the crap, junior—"

He put his hand over my mouth. "No, I mean I don't get what you want. At school, we're friendly, but you almost seem like you don't want to be around me sometimes. Then you lie down in my lap on the bus. You have to admit those are some pretty mixed signals."

"You're my friend. You are, Mikey." I didn't say anything for a few moments. "Maybe that's because I'm still trying to figure out whether we're supposed to be friends or something more. But I don't want to lose you as a friend." I thought for a minute. "I can't."

"Me neither." His voice was barely above a whisper.

I picked up his arm and tugged on it until he got the hint and climbed into my chair, into my lap. I might not have known between friend and boyfriend, but I needed to hold him, and maybe he needed to be held. I put my arms around him and rested my head on his shoulder.

"But Remy?"

"Yeah?"

"If we're friends or something else?"

"Yeah?"

"Could you at least call me Mike? Mikey's a six-year-old's name."

Chapter Five

We evidently fell asleep up on the roof, because that's where one of the chaperones found us when we were late for breakfast. We stumbled downstairs, red-faced as all of the men's squads—novice, junior varsity, and varsity—turned to face us and gave us that slow applause thing. Mikey's coach glared at him, but I could tell Lodestone was faking it, if only by the eye roll he gave me. That didn't mean I wasn't going to hear about it later, however.

Our tardiness aside, breakfast was a hurried affair because Saturday was a busy day for races. All the heats took place on Saturday, as well as repechage for the losers. Conditions could vary so much from heat to heat due to things like wind or tides, and since only the top two finishers from each heat went on to the finals, regattas that included heats typically also included a heat for the fastest of the "losers," and that was the repechage round. A two-thousand meter race might not take long—typically between six and eight minutes (and the crew better have had mechanical issues like a broken oar for that eight-minute time)—but it took a lot out of a crew, and more than one heat in a day meant rest, rehydration, and careful management of nutrition and electrolytes in between. By late morning, it wasn't unusual to find crews flopped out under their boats, half-asleep.

That's exactly what I did between my heats, only I couldn't sleep. How could I, with Mikey churning in my mind? Well, Mikey and Josh, if I were being strictly honest. All I could do was rest under the boat with my eyes closed and my earbuds in so I looked like I was out cold, but then, weren't all closeted teens masters of camouflage? Or semicloseted, in my case. I had no idea what to do, none whatsoever. I tried telling myself that I didn't have to *do* anything, that simply because Josh gave me his number didn't mean I had to call him. Likewise, just because Mikey—Mike—and I were trying to find our way, it didn't necessarily follow that we had to jump right into anything. I was almost seventeen. He would turn sixteen just before school let out for the summer. The problem was, I didn't—couldn't—listen. I felt a stress, a pressure, driving me forward.

I took the slip of paper with Josh's number out of my wallet. It was well-worn after being looked at so many times by now, but that didn't matter. I had memorized the numbers, and I could have recited them backward in my sleep. I'd even entered them in my contacts list and then password protected my phone. In fact, I'd used Josh's number as the password. That password protection more than anything might trip me up by proclaiming I had something to hide. I'd never protected my phone before, but between that number and Grindr, I didn't want Goff or anyone exploring my phone anymore. Yeah, I'd downloaded Grindr. It was all a part of my plan to see what was out there. I had no intention of setting up a profile. Not yet, at any rate, and there was no way I could've done anything at the regatta even if I hadn't been too afraid to. I didn't just have parent chaperones and coaches keeping an eye on me; I had the entire junior crew. I was even too nervous to stop by the Gay + Lesbian Rowing Federation's booth, and my crew knew I was gay. Fooling around? Ha!

But I did load Grindr once. Holy hell. My phone almost exploded.

*

I didn't sleep or play possum all the time. I watched races I wasn't in, like those of colleges I wanted to attend. Coach Lodestone told me he had been in contact with coaches at those schools all year. My performance at the Youth Nationals later this summer would clinch any deals and possibly secure an early admission or two, but I knew there had been eyes on me during the heats. Since I had not known who, when, or where, I had managed not to freak out, but it had been added pressure. If any of those coaches had joined Lodestone to watch my races, they had disappeared by the time those races ended, saving me from mortification, but only temporarily. Lodestone took me around to meet all of them.

I also watched Mikey's races. I had my eye on him, and not just because I was trying to figure out what we were to each other. I stood next to Lodestone while Mikey raced. I liked him as a person, but more important, I respected him as a coach. Then there was the undeniable hotness factor. Okay, I came into my height early, but Lodestone? He rowed at the University of Washington, and the Huskies grow them big up there or something. Lodestone was not only way over six feet tall, but Goff once told me Lodestone looked more like he was built for certain positions in football that took bulk and muscles than for crew, which needed lean strength. I mean, his shoulders were out to there. Also, he was hairy in all the right places, like beard-shadow-right-after-shaving hairy. It was awesome. He was also straight as a plank. The only thing that kept me from hating his girlfriend was that she was not only brilliant, but she was sweet as she was smart. I mean, she was deaf, and I'd started learning some basic sign language—she was that beautiful a person. Or I had that big a case of hero worship for my coach. It could've gone either way.

Lodestone watched the races and didn't acknowledge my presence. I didn't take it personally. This was his job, after all. "Do your prerace walk while you were waiting for the trailer?" he said eventually.

At least he knew I was there. I lived for these moments with my coach. It felt like he treated me as an equal, even if only for a little while. "Coach. Please."

He laughed. "What was I thinking? Of course, you did."

"And dragged most of my boat along for the ride. Something new this year though."

"Oh?" He finally glanced down at me.

"Cisco dragged Mikey and some of the other junior varsity with us."

Lodestone didn't say anything for a moment. "Interesting. What do you think they got out of it?"

I glanced at my watch and then checked the schedule. I looked out at the water, squinting through the glare of the afternoon sun. There they were. There he was. "He's varsity next year."

"Oh, you think so, do you, Coach Babcock?" Lodestone said, laughing.

I flushed. "No, seriously. If you haven't watched him on the ergs, you're falling down on the job—"

"Strong words, oarsman."

I stood my ground. "They're true, sir. His numbers have dropped steadily this season. At the same time, his erg technique has improved. He's a match for anyone on our squad."

"Ergs don't float." Lodestone's voice was quiet, almost too quiet, like he was getting angry or I'd just overstepped my bounds, but dammit, he was the one who'd encouraged me to watch and analyze other rowers. If he didn't like the results, he had only himself to blame.

"No, they don't, but boats do, and you're watching his *right now*, same as me. Tell me you don't see someone who's better than most of his boat," I said, "and he's in the A boat."

Lodestone stayed silent, watching the rest of the race through binoculars. I didn't have any, so I could only follow Mikey until they passed beyond my ability to make out any useful detail.

"Perhaps I was too hasty in my dismissal," Lodestone said, dropping his binoculars at last. "You've given this a lot of thought, and more importantly, you've been watching his form." He eyed me appraisingly. "And here I thought you'd just been watching his body."

I turned red, and not just red, scalded lobster red. Even as a kid, I had blushed hard. "Guess you heard?"

"You could say that." Lodestone put his arm across my shoulder, laughing. He had a ready laugh, at least with me. "Remy, if you don't want anyone to know, you shouldn't cuddle on the team bus. Then there was breakfast this morning. If it's any consolation, the entire girls' team thinks it's adorable. The boys' team is a bit more divided. Varsity backs you, like it always has. Junior varsity? That's another issue, but word on the street is there's more than one rower who's simply jealous."

"Aww, jeez." I had only thought I couldn't be any more embarrassed. "Wait...of who, me or Mikey?"

Lodestone snickered. "Like I'd tell you. Just enjoy it, okay? That's part of the fun of being young. Now, about your outspoken advocacy..."

"Hey, you taught me to watch other rowers and made me ride in launches to observe," I said.

"Yes, but I never thought it'd come back to bite me in the ass this soon."

*

The rest of the weekend passed in a blur of lactic acid and fatigue. The ladies' crews fared well, and while two of the three gentlemen's boats advanced from their heats, we were handed our asses in the finals. Some of it was the weather, which had turned overnight, some of it was our boys getting sick, and some of it we were just overmatched. What that might have done to my chances at recruitment, I couldn't say, but by the end of the weekend, I was too tired to overthink it. I knew Lodestone was disappointed, but the fact was we rowed the best races we had in us. Sure, we were let down, who wouldn't be? But we had no regrets, and that was the important thing. Mikey's junior varsity boat placed second for their cup. He kept muttering that second place meant first loser, and I made a note to myself to cut that off at the ankles as soon as I had a chance. That kind of talk was poison.

As it turned out, between the chaos of de-rigging and loading the trailer and then piling on the buses and hitting the road, I didn't have the chance for some time. We ended up avoiding sitting with each other. As it turned out, that bothered me. Were we friends or not? If so, why the hell weren't we sitting together? The messed-up part of it was that we spent the trip firing texts at each other. It would've been easier if we'd just sat next to each other.

Then there was all the eye-fucking. Jeez, we were stupid.

REMY: *Lodestone told me there was a bunch of people on your squad who were jelly of one of us.*

MICHAEL: *WHO???*

REMY: *He wouldn't tell me :-/*

MICHAEL: *A-hole*

REMY: *IKR?*

MICHAEL: *We should've sat together and then looked around 2 see who gave us the stink eye.*

REMY: *Too late now unless we want 2 cause more talk.*

MICHAEL: *I don't care.*

REMY: *Me neither.*

MICHAEL: *You wanna?*

I got up and evicted Mikey's seatmate with the excuse of needing Mikey's help with my History Day project. I got a notebook out and turned the overhead light on for effect because I'm sneaky that way. Not that I ended up looking at it or anything.

"Hi," I whispered as I got comfortable.

He looked at me, his eyes soft. "Hi."

I nudged my leg up against his. I was too tired to try for subtlety, but he didn't seem to mind.

We never even looked around. Mikey fell asleep, head on my shoulder. It didn't take me long to join him.

That's what came of exhausting ourselves for forty-eight hours, I guess.

*

The problem with falling asleep was that I didn't study. The problem with the timing of the Crew Classic in early April was that those of us in our junior year had barely a month's lull in school before we took the last set of exams before AP tests and then finals. Maybe the junior varsity didn't need to worry too much about AP tests, but I sure did. Those tests made a difference for me. Same with my grades. This was the last hurrah for me because the results of both would determine which colleges I could apply to and would have a chance of getting into. My less than stellar grades sophomore year needed papering over. I ate stress for all three meals each day after the Crew Classic, and it didn't stop until school let out. I swore I lived on acid blockers. Fortunately, the Crew Classic was the last regatta of the school year, and Lodestone knew the score. The juniors on the gentlemen's crew didn't exactly coast, but the intensity wasn't what it had been for me, at least until school ended.

As much as possible, I put all thoughts of Mikey, relationships, Josh, and my plan on the back burner. I'm not sure Mikey understood why, but right then, I didn't care. I couldn't. Goff was lucky. Laurel was in the same boat he and I were, and the three of us turned our dining room into a homework gulag. Mom and Dad were good sports about it too. They kept the house quiet as a tomb for us and put all thoughts of entertaining on hold so we didn't have to move anything out of the dining room. We did our best to repay them by keeping the mess under control and removing anything related to tests and projects we had finished, and by expressing our earnest gratitude for any and all homemade food. I know teenagers had the rep for being selfish, self-centered, and immature, and there was truth to that, but I'd like to think the three of us showed our better selves to Mom and Dad during that high-stress time.

Finally, the school year and regular rowing season ended, and not long after that, Goff and I turned seventeen. Then the hard work began. Some of us on the Cap City junior crew, myself included, had qualified for the Youth National Championships, so summer break? Sure, I'd be taking a class at City College, but I'd be logging many, many meters in a single without worrying about the fuss and bother of school. I just kept telling myself this was a once-in-a-lifetime opportunity, but between crew and a summer job at the boathouse, I should've forwarded my mail to the port, because I would see more of the Cap City boathouse than I would the Babcock house.

Mikey and I met up for lunch about a week after school got out. I think we both slept that entire week, save for a few text messages.

"So, what's the plan for this summer?" Mikey asked over Chinese food.

I shrugged. "Not much of one, really. SAT prep to boost my scores. A class at City College to pad my college applications and make next year a little easier. And, oh yeah, sculling until Lodestone takes pity on me and puts me out of my misery. You?"

Mikey snorted. "Which means never. He won't rest until you're standing on the podium at the Nationals."

I groaned and slumped down in my seat. Mikey responded by kicking me under the table. "None of that. You know you want it just as much, or you wouldn't put up with it."

"Ow." I rubbed my shins. "You've got sharp toes."

He rolled his eyes. "Suck it. What're you taking at City College?"

"US Government. It's required and it's only a semester, so I might as well get it over with. You?" But him telling me to suck it? So not the thing to say, especially since I had seen him in the showers, because that was exactly where my mind went.

"US History," he said around a mouth full of sweet and sour chicken. Keep it classy there, Mikey.

"No AP History?"

He shrugged. "I'd rather get it over with this summer, and I can still take the AP test."

"Good point. I kind of wish I'd done that, now you mention it." I thought about it some more. "It might've made last year easier."

"That's kind of what I'm hoping after watching you. You seemed pretty stressed."

Stressed did not even begin to cover it, but it was not all academics. How could I tell him what I really wanted to do was lure him into a dark corner? And that was new. I'd need to examine that sometime, maybe after I was done examining him.

Talk turned away from academics to rowing. Big surprise, since we both had it bad. We made plans to get up early in the morning and scull, and by early we meant 7:00 a.m. or so. That gave us time before classes started. It was also what passed for a relaxed summer in education-obsessed Davis.

It would make for a pleasant few weeks, at least until Cap City's various learn-to-row camps started, along with the ongoing adaptive rowing clinics. Lodestone had asked me to help coach the junior crew's learn-to-row, but I'd already been tapped by Coach Sundstrom to help with his adaptive program, and that would be my summer job. Besides, Lodestone pretty much owned my ass as it was, since the only way I wouldn't embarrass myself at the Youth Nationals would be long hours in a single while he cracked a whip, possibly literally.

Once camp, classes, and SAT prep started, I'd be busier than a one-armed fan dancer. I kept telling myself it would be a *different* kind of busy than the school year. Sometimes I thought my delusions were the only thing pulling me through. I wished I could have said that Goff was the smart one, but he planned to spend his summer the same way. The only difference was that he followed a different schedule—SAT prep in the morning, followed by working out and classes in the afternoon, and his job in the evening.

The summer looked to be a long one.

Chapter Six

Summer classes at City College had started the week before, and already Mikey and I had midterms to study for. That was the joy of compressed summer sessions. Neither of us wanted to face any of the libraries that were open, so one Thursday we opted for my house, specifically my bedroom. We curled up on my bed, head to toe, bracketed by the head- and footboards. Mikey wrapped his arm around my feet, and I wrapped mine around his. We were cozy and studying. With snacks and drinks within easy reach, we were set for the afternoon. Since the subject matter overlapped—American government and the first half of the US history sequence—we took turns quizzing each other.

I guess it looked suspiciously like sixty-nine, but neither of us went there. Goff must've, however, because when he barged in without knocking, he stopped dead. "Oh. I didn't... That is, I—"

I looked up from my notes, mildly annoyed by the interruption. "Yes?"

By that time Goff had turned bright red. "I didn't mean to interrupt anything, guys. I'm sorry. I didn't know you two were—"

"Studying?" Mikey said, one eyebrow arched, clearly amused.

I seriously thought my brother was going to swallow his tongue. "Uh...yeah. Studying."

"Is there something I can help you with?" I said.

Goff—or should I have called him Goof?—looked relieved. "I'm heading to work, but the car's low on gas. If I leave you a twenty and take the scooter, will you promise not to hate me?"

In addition to the car, our parents had also bought us a Vespa to share, figuring that between the two we could and would make it work.

"Sure, no sweat. Thanks for the warning. I may bike to SAT prep tonight and then gas the car up tomorrow on the way to the port if that's okay. I'll drop it off before class."

Goff looked relieved. "I just didn't want to leave you in the lurch with a car low on gas. See you guys later."

Mikey and I waited until his footsteps faded and then burst out laughing. "You realize he thinks we're dating, right?" Mikey said.

I nodded, still snickering. "That look on his face? Priceless."

"I guess I'm out to him," I said. "Or he thinks I am."

"How do you feel about that?"

The thought frightened me, but also relieved me a little. Of course, this assumed he hadn't heard anything around school, which as I thought about it had to be a near-impossibility. "I'd have to tell him sooner or later, but honestly? I've hated keeping it from him. But just because you and I are affectionate doesn't mean we're together."

"True."

I went back to my studying, but I felt Mikey's eyes on me before he picked up his book. Then I started thinking about us, about our dancing around the possibility of actually dating, along with our affection toward each other on the trip to San Diego. We had certainly been an item, even if only an item of confusion. We never figured out who we had made jealous, but my feelings where Mikey was concerned were still conflicted.

I looked back up at him. "You ever think about being together? Going out, I mean."

"Yeah." Mikey closed his book and met my eyes. He had the most amazing hazel eyes. How come I had never noticed that? "But I'm saving myself for the right guy at the right time if that makes sense."

And apparently that wasn't me, despite our weekend in San Diego, despite everything that led up to it. Apparently, it had all been in my head. Given my pre-Crew Classic ambivalence about being out and about with Mikey, I couldn't figure out why I felt like he'd just kicked me in the stomach. But that's what it felt like—like I should be vomiting blood.

I faked a smile. "Me too, I guess."

"Remy, are you okay?"

I smiled at Mikey and forced myself to meet his eyes. "Why wouldn't I be?"

"Just checking."

We both went back to our studying, but there was a weird current in the air. Uh...duh?

"So," I said eventually, "did I ever tell you what happened while we were de-rigging for the Crew Classic?"

"No, as a matter of fact, you didn't. You been holding out on me?"

I snorted. "You could say that. Some guy came up to me wanting information about the adaptive rowing program."

Mikey thought for a moment. "As I recall, you were about half-dressed while you were de-rigging the double for Coach Lodestone. I can't wait to hear how this sorted out."

"Dude, we were all half-dressed."

"The girls weren't half-dressed."

"Whatever. Do you want to hear about this?"

"Yes, I think I do."

So, I started in on Stranger Guy's story. "Anyway, after I told him where to find the adaptive-rowing info, I looked up from de-rigging, and he was just leaning against the boathouse staring at me." I shook my head at the memory, hoping I could hide the wood I felt growing.

"Are you serious?" Mikey said. "You didn't show him yourself?"

"Of course not, I was de-rigging a boat." I shook my head. Honestly, where did he get this stuff?

"Was he hot?" Mikey asked.

"Totally."

Mikey leaned forward and smacked my forehead.

"Ouch! What was that for?" I rubbed the spot he'd smacked.

"Because a hot guy asked you for directions and then turned and watched you, and *you kept de-rigging a boat*. You're hopeless."

Was he for real? "Okay, so what should I have done?"

"Followed him? Offered to help him out?" Mikey sighed. He gave me a funny look; one I couldn't decipher. His eyes looked bright, but he wasn't crying. Whatever. Why did people have to be so confusing? I realized then that I would never figure Mikey out.

"Okay, but with what? I'd already given him perfectly clear directions to the singles house, and I'm pretty sure that's where Coach Bedford keeps the adaptive rowing program."

"Oh, for the love of... You know, for someone who's so desperate to get laid, you sure are dense," Mikey snapped. "To answer your question, anything he wanted."

I guess Mikey was right, but what I failed to understand was his attitude. He stared at me like he was sad but also kind of angry. What the hell? He literally just shot me down for a relationship or even casual dating. One of these years, I might learn to keep my mouth shut, because apparently no good ever came of me talking. Boats made so much more sense.

What confused me the most, however, was Mikey's vibe. I'd never felt this kind of hostility from him.

*

There was a wonderful '80s band called Toy Matinee. It produced only a single eponymous album, and the band never received the attention it deserved, at least in my opinion. But with tracks devoted to Vaclav Havel, Salvador Dali, and Madonna? I was all over it. I lived my life through '80s music. Why think when I could find a lyric to express an idea for me? Toy Matinee wrote very intelligent lyrics. No wonder they didn't last long. "Last Plane Out," the one song that got any airplay, contained a lyric that held special meaning for me: "Greetings from Sodom, how we wish you were here..." Actually, I thought the entire song was brilliant, but that part especially. *Greetings from Sodom!* I could see it on a postcard. There was also a song on the album called "There Was a Little Boy," and one line in particular jumped out at me: "...he finds what he needs with an older boy," and it looked like that would be coming to pass for me.

Yep, I was going to call Josh. Eventually. As soon as I found my balls, because the entire thought scared the crap out of me. But what had been the purpose, I asked myself over and over, of keeping his number—let alone entering it into my phone—if I never intended to use it? I could say whatever I wanted about a lifeline to the one adult gay man I knew of, but couldn't I just as easily have gone and bought a copy of *Instinct* or *DNA* or *Out* or something? I didn't think those were kept behind counters or anything like that. But maybe those weren't the same, and I was just stalling.

So, I set myself a deadline of when I would call Josh because otherwise, I knew I never would. I promised myself that I would call him the following Monday, which made it four days after Mikey went rogue on me and allowed me to get through my midterm without thinking about any of it. Compartmentalization was my friend. The only problem was once I had finished my exam. Then I faced a weekend of adaptive rowing while ignoring Mikey and strange looks from Lodestone, to say nothing of Goff.

"Where's Mikey?" Goff said. We were standing in the kitchen on Sunday afternoon, the only time we were both free at the same time all week.

How was I supposed to explain to Goff that what he had seen not only didn't mean what he thought it did, but also that I had done something—I didn't know what—to alienate Mikey? Thinking about it still stung.

"At home, I guess."

"I thought you two were…"

"Were what, Goff?" I looked at him with wide-eyed, vacuous innocence. I didn't intend to make this easy on him.

"Were, uh…you know," he said urgently.

"No, I really don't."

Turning redder by the second, Goff grabbed my arm, dragged me out of the kitchen, and threw me into the downstairs bathroom, closing the door behind us. Then he switched on the fan, just to cover anything we said.

"You know damn well what I mean, *Germy*. I walked in, and you two were crawling all over each other."

"We were not." I laughed. "We were *studying*. If you think that's sex, Laurel must be very frustrated. Also, why do I keep buying you condoms?"

"Don't try to distract me." Goff shoved me against the door.

"Damn, that hurt! Knock it off," I said, pushing him back.

Goff held up his hands. "Okay, I'm sorry. I didn't mean to hurt you, okay?"

It was a good thing Goff hadn't meant to hurt me. I'd hate to feel intentional damage. I had forgotten just how strong my brother was. I rubbed the back of my head where it had hit the door. "Next time you want my attention, just rack me, okay? It won't hurt as much."

"I said I was sorry."

I sighed. I had no idea why we were even going through this farce. Goff had to know the answer to what he was asking. I mean, how could he not? "What do you really want to know?"

Like I couldn't have guessed.

"Remy...are you gay?"

I looked at him closely. He looked miserable, and that was one thing I hadn't expected. I glanced at the floor. Somehow, I couldn't look my brother in the face. "Yeah, I think I am," I said softly.

"You know it's okay, right? With me, I mean?"

My throat felt thick, and it was hard to breathe, like I was starting to cry. I didn't want to cry. I didn't want to talk about this. I didn't want to be gay, even though I knew I was. I hadn't chosen this, but right at that moment, it didn't matter. It set me apart from everyone I knew, everyone but Mikey, and he wasn't speaking to me.

I jumped when I felt him touch my face, but Goff lifted my chin up so he could see my eyes. "It's okay."

"How can you say that?" I said thickly. "You're not gay. You don't have to worry about Mom and Dad freaking out. Your future is what you think it will be. Mine? I have to face losing everyone."

I heard him sniffle. "Not me. You'll always have me."

Then he grabbed me and held me. I hesitated, but then I hugged him back. I didn't know how long we were in the bathroom sobbing into each other's shoulders, but it didn't matter. That's why we had each other.

"Thanks," I said when I looked up at last.

He snickered. "Guess I should've listened when you said you really weren't interested in Laurel."

"Jackass." I shoved him. Then I glanced in the mirror. "We look awful. Neither of us has the coloring for this."

Goff laughed weakly. "You're horrible."

"I know." I hesitated. "Thanks, Goff. You don't know how much this means to me."

"I think I do. You've had my back for so long. I've been waiting to have yours." Goff paused. "You seem like you're made of ice, like you don't need anyone, but it's not true, is it?"

I shook my head. "No, but when you're hiding something..."

"No hiding anymore. You've got me and Mikey, and I know for a fact Laurel won't care. She's said as much—"

"Mikey and I aren't together, remember?" I laughed. What else could I do?

"Really? But I saw—"

"I know, but we're just friends, I promise. Or I think we *were* friends. I'm not sure what's going on. We were pretty tight at the Crew Classic, and I honestly thought we were heading for more, but turned out I was wrong." That cut like a knife, and I was tired of it, but I didn't have the first clue what to do. Pounding on his door was out since Mikey had made his feelings clear. So was imitating John Cusack in that '80s movie in which he stood outside his love interest's house blasting some Peter Gabriel song on an impossibly large tape player, if only because I didn't make a fool out of myself very well.

Goff looked at me through narrowed eyes. "But why's he mad at you?"

"I really don't know, and I'm too tired to care right now. It'll sort itself out or it won't, but I do know one thing..."

"Yeah?"

I nodded. "If he wants to row this summer, he'll pull the stick out of his butt. He's too young for a key to the boathouse."

Goff laughed. "You were always a practical one."

"Guilty as charged, I guess." Then something occurred to me. "We've been in here long enough to raise suspicions."

"I guess, but we really don't talk like this anymore, do we?"

I would never have expected Goff to say something like that, but maybe that only showed how long it had been since my brother and I had shared anything. "I'll try to be more open in the future."

Goff cocked his head. "You think it's because—"

"The closet wraps everything in secrets. I have to think about everything I say. It's a relief that you know." It was too.

"What about Mom and Dad?"

I shook my head. "I have to tell them in my own time." I shuddered, and not for effect. "Can you imagine Dad's response? He can barely stand me as it is."

"Remy..." Goff looked so sad. "That's not true. You can't say things like that."

"You've always gotten along better with them than I have, especially Dad. You know that. Just...please don't say anything."

"They won't hear it from me." I could tell he was troubled by what I'd said, but it was the truth and it always had been. He'd never wanted to see it, and I hated bringing it up. He was the one person in the world I was closest to. I never did understand why some people didn't get along with their brothers or sisters, but then, I bought my brother condoms, so we clearly had an unusual relationship in the first place.

Just before we left the bathroom, Goff elbowed me. "So, if you and Mikey aren't an item, I guess I won't have any competition for the rubbers."

"It's not looking that way, is it?"

*

Monday came and went, and naturally, I never called Josh. I was too busy chewing my liver out about the entire thing. I knew I had a reputation for ice water in place of blood and nerves of steel. I'd heard it from Goff and Mikey, among others. But a lot of it was talk. A good rep meant a lot of avoided nonsense, but I had always liked to imagine there'd been a bit of truth to it. So where was that kernel? It was Friday night right before SAT prep, and I only had flop sweat to show for my efforts. That was me, a legend in my own mind.

Okay, enough was more than enough. I pulled out my phone.

REMY: *Hey, remember me? It's Remy from the Cap City Boathouse. I gave you directions.*

Then I turned my phone off and spent the next two hours learning how to boost my SAT scores.

Chapter Seven

Oh, Josh remembered me, all right. First of all, my phone lit up—lit up like Times Square on New Year's Eve—when I turned it back on after class. *Buzz buzz buzz!* with a bunch of incoming text messages.

> JOSH: *Hey, pretty, of course I remember U ;-)*
>
> …
>
> JOSH: *U there?*
>
> …
>
> JOSH: *Text me back, brah.*

My hands shook as I read them. Crap. I should have told him I was going to be in class. This was what I'd wanted, right? So why was it so hard to breathe? By that point I figured I should just wait until I got home to reply. It wasn't like I had any hot plans for the night. Goff probably did so I was pretty sure I'd be left alone, especially if I told our parents I had to study. That wouldn't have even been a lie. I always had to study. And sleep.

I couldn't remember the ride home. I guess I hadn't done anything stupid since I made it home alive. I fixed a snack and took it upstairs with me, and then cleaned up. As I suspected, Goff was in the bathroom at the same time.

"You're getting ready for bed?" He sounded surprised.

What could I say? "It's been a long day."

"Did you just whine?" He nudged me with his shoulder.

"Probably. All I want to do is crawl under the covers and sleep for a week." At this point, I probably couldn't have slept even with a face full of sedatives. I wanted to do something under the covers all right, but as close as Goff and I were, there were some things we did not share. "Unfortunately, I have to be up bright and early and ready to scull until I achieve perfection, and then help with a learn-to-row clinic I was drafted into."

I must have made a face, because Goff gave me a look of purest concern. "I thought you liked luring innocent young lads and lasses into a life of torture and rowing."

"This is an adult learn-to-row clinic, actually." I had to smile at Goff's phrasing, because he was right. "I'm just doing it because I get paid. One of the masters coaches is in charge. I'm just driving a boat."

"You're coxing?" Goff laughed. "This I have to see."

"You know where the boathouse is. Come watch."

"Don't you get too far out on the water to see much?"

I'd taken my contacts out by this time, so I looked over my glasses at him. "First day. We won't get that far," I muttered darkly.

I could tell by his smile that he was thinking about it. "Can I bring Laurel?"

"Of course." I gave him a look. He knew how much I liked her. "The more the merrier. If the water's calm, you might even be able to hear me doing a bad job of keeping my temper. The real fun, however, will be the coaches trying to do the same thing, and they'll have powered megaphones. You'll hear them loud and clear."

Goff pulled out his phone. "I'm telling Laurel about this right now."

"The more I think about this, the more it says something sad about us all that this is the most entertaining thing we can come up with." I shook my head.

"Remy, we're under eighteen. We can't drink, we can't get into clubs—okay, you and I can, but our friends can't—and we're not the type to spend the summer stoned. Let's face it, Davis in the summer is quieter than a grave. Watching you not blowing your stack, or better yet, not screaming and swimming for shore? Best game in town."

I had to admit Goff was right. It just sucked to hear it put so bluntly. "Okay, there's nothing I can say to that, but Goff?"

"Yeah?"

"Don't you dare wear as much aftershave as you're pouring into your hand. Some on the cheeks, some further south, and that's it. The idea is to make her go hunting for that elusive scent, not to choke us all in a cloud of it."

I was the recipient of the one-fingered mudra of contempt, but he poured about half of it down the drain and then followed directions. "Why am I taking advice from a gay virgin?"

"Because I'm right," I said around my toothbrush.

"And that's the most annoying part. Sleep well, Germy, don't wait up." And with that, my brother finished dressing. Then he was out of the door and I had the bathroom to myself.

I padded back into my bedroom and locked my door. This wasn't something I wanted company for.

I climbed into bed and pulled out my phone. I didn't see any point to putting it off. I mean, I'd already jerked Josh's chain enough.

> REMY: *Sorry, not ignoring U on purpose. In class this evening*

Josh responded almost immediately.

> JOSH: *Ah, the joys of summer school. Whatcha taking?*

Damn. He would ask. What would they call US government at UCD?

REMY: *Poli sci. Just basic US government*

JOSH: *Were we a bad boy and flunked poli sci 1a?*

I started getting over my fear. The weird thing was, I was pretty into it already.

REMY: *If I say yes, will you punish me?*

JOSH: *Whoa. Don't waste any time, do U ;-)*

REMY: *Did I mistake your intentions when U were eye-fucking me at the boathouse?*

Josh didn't reply right away. Maybe I had misread him. I was about to apologize when he texted back.

JOSH: *Sorry. Had to ditch roommates. No U weren't wrong. Wanted to nail you against wall then&there*

REMY: *Could tell*

He was killing me with this.

JOSH: *So. Wanna meet?*

REMY: *When/where?*

JOSH: *Tomorrow?*

I thought about that. My Saturdays were pretty busy, but I could probably get away after dinner. Studying—my eternal excuse.

REMY: *I have 2 study, so library?*

JOSH: *Perfect. Shields?*

Shields was the main library at UC Davis. Despite a renovation in the '90s, it was still a labyrinth, full of dark corners and out-of-the-way bathrooms. I could only imagine what Josh had in mind.

REMY: *I can be there by 7*

JOSH: *Meet U on 3rd floor by men's room. Wear uni?*

REMY: *Yes 2 meet no 2 uni*

JOSH: *Buzzkill*

REMY: *Goodnight, Romeo*

JOSH: *LOL C U 2morrow*

*

Late the next night, I shut my bedroom door behind me and leaned against it. I managed not to slam it, but only just. Goff had taken Laurel to the movies, and my parents were asleep. I'm surprised my heart pounding in my chest didn't wake them up.

I couldn't believe I had done what I had just done. My head spun from it all, and I needed to talk to someone desperately. Even if he hadn't been busy, I was not sure this was something I could share with my brother. He had my back, but this involved my front. I did not need to know what he and Laurel did with theirs; he probably didn't want to know what I did with mine. That left one person I could talk to.

Mikey.

One problem with that.

Either he or I was going to have to suck it up and call the other one. Suck. Maybe that was a poor choice of words in the present circumstances, but dammit, I needed to debrief with my best friend or former best friend or best enemy or whatever he was, especially since I would probably see Josh around the boathouse when he was helping out with the adaptive rowing program in some capacity or other.

And because I knew this—I would hook up with Josh again.

So, it looked like I would be texting Mikey, even though I was not the one who went psycho.

> REMY: *I called Stranger Guy. I really need to talk.*

And then what? Suddenly I didn't know what to do with myself. I knew there would be no way I could focus long enough to study, either US government or SAT prep. I took a shower for lack of anything better to do. Maybe that would relax me enough to sleep.

When I got out, Mikey had blown up my phone, and I breathed a sigh of relief. A huge sigh. An epic sigh. Never mind the shower, the fact that Mikey still cared enough to reply relaxed me.

> MICHAEL: *Where are you? You can't just say things like that and disappear.*

> REMY: *Shower. Can U meet? Would U rather text?*

> MICHAEL: *Can U come over here?*

> REMY: *B there ASAP.*

I texted Goff where I was going and then pushed the Vespa down the block before I started it. It occurred to me that my brother and I barely told our parents anything but stayed in almost constant contact with each other. It was a twin thing, and Mom and Dad had learned to work with that. If they wanted to know where one of us was, they asked the other.

When I got to Mikey's house, he had already opened his bedroom window and removed the screen. His parents had to know what the ladder on the side of the house was for—didn't they?—but either they didn't mind or they were truly clueless. Regardless, I had other things on my mind, and quick and lithe as a cat, I was up and in Mikey's room in moments.

I'd barely set my feet on the carpet before he grabbed my arm and pulled me over to his bed. "Well?"

"Hello to you too."

He waved that away. "Yeah yeah yeah, I missed you. We've kissed and made up. Now start talking."

I started at the beginning with the texting—why revealing what a chickenshit I was mattered, I didn't know, and besides, he probably already knew—but a part of me thought that if Mikey hadn't been such a psycho, we wouldn't—figuratively speaking—have had to kiss and make up, and could be in a relationship of our very own already, and might therefore actually have been kissing.

"So, we met tonight."

"Ohmygod where?" Mikey gasped.

"Shields Library."

His jaw dropped. "He nailed you in a bathroom?"

"No, he didn't nail me," I said testily, "and lower your voice, unless you want your parents listening in." Honestly, this would've gone so much better if he'd just let me talk. "Can I just finish this?"

"Go on, go on, but this is killing me. Talk faster."

And my nerves were back. "I don't know how I made it through today. I was a nervous wreck. I mean, scared all day—"

"You? Scared?" Mikey laughed. "That's novel."

"Yeah, me. Scared. Any more clever remarks? Can I continue?" Maybe Mikey didn't know me that well after all.

Mikey made a "keep talking" gesture with his hand. "Yes, scared all day, and it got worse the closer I got, like I was going to puke the entire bike ride to campus. I almost turned around every time I stopped at a stop sign or red light. Even once I was in the library, I thought about bailing."

I looked up at Mikey, expecting to see him laughing or something, but he only looked concerned. "By the time I found where Josh said to meet, I felt like I was going to pass out." I sighed. "But I did it. I actually did it. I held another man's dick in my hand. He held mine."

"And?" Mikey whispered.

I laughed. It almost sounded bitter to my ears. "And I'm doing it again. It's way better than whacking off."

"But that's all you did, mutual j/o?"

I nodded. "That and kissing."

"What was that like? Kissing a guy?" He looked entranced.

I leaned forward and kissed him on the lips, just a brief kiss. "Magical."

Mikey blinked. "So—" His voice cracked, and he coughed to clear it. "So, what made the difference? You almost turned around; you were so nervous you were sick to your stomach. Why'd you change your mind?"

"Josh's jaw dropped when he saw me." I smiled at the memory. Definitely a confidence builder. "Okay, I wore a tight T-shirt kinda sorta on purpose."

"You mean like the one you have on now?"

I looked down. I guess it was tight. They all fit like this one. Maybe I was growing again? "About, yeah. Maybe shorter? If I moved, you could see skin."

Mikey blushed. "Wow. Um...maybe you could show me some time. I mean, maybe Josh was nervous too."

"Could be." I wondered what Mikey was getting at. If his signals were any more mixed, he would have needed to use a blender for a transmitter. "But I guess weight training is good for more than moving boats, because he sure got off on my muscles."

"You really don't know, do you?" Mikey had a funny look on his face.

I cocked my head to one side. "Don't know what?"

"Don't worry about it, Remy. Just keep lifting so you make the boats go faster."

I knew right then that I would never understand Mikey, and possibly never understand any other man either. But that might have been okay. As I had learned that night, they seemed to like what they saw.

"You know what the best part of it was? Hands down?"

Mikey shook his head slowly.

"The exhilaration. I've never felt like that before. I can't describe the feeling of power that came from holding him, from holding Josh's dick. In that moment, I realized something. I could control him absolutely."

Mikey opened his mouth, but snapped it shut. He looked worried or something.

"What?"

He tried again. "That's...not what I expected you to say."

I shrugged. What could I say to that? I wasn't a mind reader. "I think it's time to get you a fake ID too."

"Wait, what? Too?" Mikey looked like a whiplash victim.

I nodded. "I've got a fake ID. Geoff, too, but let's leave him out of this."

"Because I look soooo mature?"

"Yeah, that part might be a bit tricky, and the photochopping could be expensive. I'll help pay for it since this is all my idea."

"Okay, now for the why?" Mikey said, his tone indicating that he was humoring the crazy man.

"So we can get you into clubs. Some of them have eighteen-and-over nights."

Mikey looked at me like I was stupid. "I want to do this...why?"

"Well Jesus H Christ, Mikey. I'll need a wingman if I'm going to find guys at clubs. I figure it's safer than online," I said. He wasn't getting it, but it was plain as daylight to me. "Then, too, you might want in on the action, amiright?"

The silence, as they say, deafened. Mikey stared at me for a long time. Like, long enough to make me squirm.

"You sicken me. Get out."

I stared at him. I could not be hearing this. "What the—?"

"Get. Out."

I stood up. "Could you please make up your mind? You want me, you don't want me, but apparently you don't like the idea of me finding anyone else either. I don't know what the hell that's about."

Mikey didn't say anything, but I'd never seen him so furious. His arms were crossed over his chest, and he was shaking he was so mad.

"You said you were saving yourself for the right guy at the right time. For a while in San Diego, I'd thought— no, I'd hoped—that was me. Then you made it clear it wasn't." I almost told him how that had hurt, but then I realized it was not any of his business, not anymore. Besides, now I was every bit as furious as he. "You can't have it both ways, you know."

And with that, I climbed out of the window. He could close it behind me.

The problem with having ridden the Vespa over was that I couldn't take my anger out on the pedals. No, I had to sit there sedately on the seat, puttering my way home. Whoever heard of taking a mad out by speeding furiously through the streets on a Vespa? No one, that's who.

But what the ever-living hell? I couldn't figure out what Mikey wanted. He'd turned me down, but he was angry—no, sickened—that I found affection somewhere else.

Whatever, Mikey. I don't need you, anyway.

Chapter Eight

After that, I found myself alone for much of the rest of the summer. Not alone, strictly speaking. I was around people all the time, whether it was in class at City College or in my SAT prep course or at the boathouse sculling balls to the wall in preparation for the Nationals, but those were alone in a crowd. No besties or anything, no one to talk to who knew me.

Mom even noticed one day. "Where is everyone?"

I looked up from my reading. "What do you mean?"

"You've never been one for a lot of friends, Remy, but you're usually with *someone*. For the last week, however, it's just been you. Is something wrong? Are you and Mikey fighting?"

She sounded really worried. "No, Mom. We're both just really busy this summer."

"I know, sweetie, but you used to study with each other. Lately it's not even that."

"I know. His summer school and my practice for Nationals and everything else don't really overlap." I couldn't really tell her the truth, but I smiled to throw her off the scent. "We'll get it all sorted out eventually. We still talk and see each other at the boathouse."

"That's something at least." She shook her head. "This overscheduling you kids do to yourselves. I never thought I'd be telling my children to slow down. Isn't it the other way around?"

I had to laugh. "Welcome to Davis."

"I know, but it's not healthy, is it?" But she laughed too.

"Probably not, but hey, college'll be easy, right?"

"It would have to be." She kissed the top of my head. "Don't forget to sleep sometime."

"I think I've got it on my schedule."

Mom shook her head. "That'd be funny if it weren't true."

Goff knew the score, so he and Laurel tried to include me in their activities, or some of them. They meant well and I loved them both for it, but who wanted to be a third wheel? I tagged along but seeing them being a couple just rubbed it in that I wasn't. Josh hardly counted.

Speaking of, Josh and I saw a fair amount of each other—under certain circumstances—and it beat doing it myself, but we weren't in any sense of the term in a relationship, and neither of us thought we were. As much as I longed for the walking-hand-in-hand, trading-letter-jackets, going-steady boyfriend, my ideas about casual changed a lot over the summer, and I realized that Mr. Right Now would do while I waited for Mr. Right.

I hadn't lied to Mom when I told her I saw Mikey at the boathouse. We just ignored each other in a painfully obvious fashion. Even Lodestone noticed it one morning before practice. He only raised an eyebrow in comment as the gentlemen's crew prepared for the morning's row.

I shook my head. "Don't ask. It's too stupid for words."

"At least you recognize it. Do I want to know?"

"Not unless you find it amusing that he doesn't want to go out but doesn't want me to see anyone else." My voice might've dripped a certain amount of contempt.

Lodestone made a face while my teammates tried to stifle their laughter.

"Yep, that about sums it up."

"So... Throwing yourself into sculling, are you?"

I raised one eyebrow. "You noticed."

"You've gotten a lot faster lately, for what it's worth."

I saluted him. "Right now? Everything."

"I'm sorry you're going through this," Lodestone said, putting a hand on my shoulder, "but if you're up for it, I'll keep doing everything I can to help you transmute this lead into gold at the Nationals."

"I'm all yours, Coach."

He smiled at me. "You always have been, you know."

"So people tell me."

Lodestone rewarded me with two hours in hell, and I loved every minute of it. I managed to keep even with the four on some of the pieces. They hated me, and they should've. There were four of them in one boat, four people and four oars. There was one of me in a tiny boat with two much smaller oars. They lumbered along. I set the water ablaze, with Cisco and Jack in a pair nipping at my heels. I'd always hated the pair. The pair was just like the big boat we'd rowed in San Diego, only a tiny slice of it—one oar per rower and not much boat. They were tippy and temperamental, and I'd rolled them before. I was at one with my single, and it showed. Lodestone wasn't shy about using me or Cisco and Jack to berate the four. We grinned at them; they gnashed their teeth.

*

SAT prep finished and I retook the SATs, raising my scores by a decent amount. Goff too. Laurel pretended ours were on par with hers, which we appreciated. She was polite that way. I doubted I would take them again after that. They had reached a respectable level, and I knew I could do only so much. My grades, my AP test scores, and my various community-college courses along with community service projects via crew and school clubs would have to make up for any deficiencies. I couldn't be all things to every admissions officer. No one could, except apparently Laurel. As I told her, it was a good thing she was beautiful inside and out, and thank goodness Goff didn't have to glower at me anymore. Now that I was out to him, he knew I wasn't putting the moves on his girlfriend.

After the prep course and the SATs were done, all that was left in my summer were twice-daily training for Nationals and my explorations of what my dick was good for. As it turned out, it was good for all kinds of good times. I was reasonably discriminating within the bounds of being young and having fun. It's not like I had turned into a tomcat or anything. I kept my dignity, but as I had the time or the urge, I went looking.

Josh and I continued our discreet encounters, and we both had fun, but that was all it ever was—fun. So, I branched out because I wanted to have *more* fun. I nosed around some of the quote, unquote gay dating sites, but they were only dating sites if you wanted your dates to last an hour or less. Adams2Steves.com struck me as the best game around insofar as everyone there admitted it was a game and played accordingly. I put up a profile, lying through my electronic teeth about age and everything related to that sort of thing. The one thing I insisted on was "drug and disease free/UB2." I never replied to messages unless the profile stated that. Mine did, and I expected that in my playmates. A lot of guys around my alleged age seemed to have time on their hands during the summer, mostly college students I presumed, since that was what I appeared to be. They were there when I wanted them, and that was what mattered.

I'd never deleted Grindr from my phone after San Diego, and that turned out to be a great source for college guys. There was something oddly compelling about it too.

It felt like walking into a store. I could point to anyone and say, "Yes, shopkeeper, I'll have that one." And I could. Josh had taught me that much. I apparently checked off a lot of guys' boxes. I didn't think I was all that special, just some guy who looked older than he was through an accident of heredity and who happened to be built up through his choice of recreational pastime/obsession. People couldn't help how old they looked, but anyone who felt like putting the time in could make the most of what he or she had. That struck me as fairly democratic, and who knew how long rowing would hold my interest? I mean, it wasn't a varsity sport at most colleges anymore and hadn't been for years. If I got to college and couldn't sustain my studies and crew, there could be only one choice of which I'd vote off the island. I could always pick crew back up after I graduated. But if I didn't row? I knew I'd be about as active as a rock, and then I wouldn't look like I did, and presumably the interest on Grindr would dry up.

Goff knew I slipped out at night on occasion, but then again, so did he. I suppose he thought I'd met someone, and since I'd always been fairly closemouthed, he didn't seem to think too much of it. I didn't burden him with the details that I'd met several someones and rarely saw them more than once or twice. What was the point? It's not like I could date any of these men. If they found out I was in high school, they'd panic. If my parents found out I was seeing someone in college, they'd freak out. They didn't even know I was gay. It was a bad situation all the way around, and I knew it. I couldn't really face the thought of telling my parents and trying to make it better, however. There was no point, since Mikey had already rejected me, but damn, I had thought coming out to Goff would have put an end to the secrets between us.

Then complications ensued with Josh. Ensued? More like exploded. I was just glad I escaped injury from the hot shrapnel.

One afternoon before practice, I was putting my single in slings. Something had been off with one of the riggers during the morning practice, and I refused to go through another practice with a gimpy rigger.

A shadow fell across the boat, blocking my sight. I looked up, irritated and ready to rip into whomever it was, only to see Josh. I smiled instead.

"Hey, pretty," he said. He wore street clothes, so I assumed he was here to do something related to his internship with the adaptive rowing program rather than to work out or row.

"What's up?" I stretched the slight crick in my back. Why the slings for singles had to be so low to the ground I would never know, but given that the sport selected for reasonably tall people even at the juniors level, I failed to see why equipment manufacturers couldn't scale things up a bit.

Then I noticed his neck and stopped hearing a single word he said. Red blotches everywhere. He looked like he'd been attacked by an Electrolux or mauled by a Hoover.

I must have made the right responses back because he continued on to wherever he was going. The moon? Hell? It could have been anywhere, but my vote was for hell.

I knew Josh and I weren't exclusive. We had never discussed it, for starters, and I was hardly the poster boy for monogamy. Josh and I had also never dated in any formal sense of the term, if only because dating traditionally took place in locations other than public bathrooms, as hot as that could be. Even I knew that much about actual dating, despite Mikey's probably realistic assumptions about my fixed focus on crew to the exclusion of everything else.

That wasn't what had made my jaw shatter on the floor.

It was the total lack of discretion. Under the circumstances, I valued discretion highly. It was a courtesy I gave to Josh and expected in return. While closeted in many areas of my life and thus practiced at hiding, I was new to all of this relationship business, even a relationship as casual as the one I thought I shared with Josh, and so disguising emotions when my first and current flaunted the evidence of another inamorato in front of me took more skill than I possessed right then, not with everything else demanding my attention.

I must have stared after him for a good five minutes.

"Hey, Remy," Lodestone said when he walked into the boathouse. When I didn't reply, he said, "Are you okay?"

That snapped me back to myself. That was exactly what I needed—a test of my emotional fortitude in front of a coach as perceptive and intelligent as Peter Lodestone.

"What? Oh. Hi, Coach." I blushed. Could I be any dopier? "I'm fine. Just lost in space."

He frowned at me. "Is everything all right?"

"Yep, just some trouble with one of the riggers, but I've about got it fixed."

I went back to work, but I felt Lodestone's eyes on me the entire time. Even when I left, I was sure he watched me all the way down the dock.

*

I spent my free time for the next several days hooking up with guys I found on Grindr, like it was some sort of payback to Josh for his infidelity. Only I didn't tell him because I was being discreet. How was that for messed-up logic? What I had not realized was that I had not left my distraction on the dock and that Lodestone had been connecting the dots. In other words, as usual, I failed to notice anything. When something bothered me, I just sculled longer and harder. But one afternoon at practice a few days later—those of us going to Nationals were well into two practices a day by then—I noticed Josh talking to Lodestone on the dock. I saw the two of them grow increasingly agitated. I heard voices but did not and honestly could not care. I was about as emotionless as a block of wood at that point.

I stopped sculling and watched them. Then I saw Lodestone grab—literally grab—Coach Sundstrom and drag him into the argument, because by that time I'd figured out they were fighting. I assumed the only reason it hadn't turned physical was because Lodestone could've folded Josh into a pretzel and Sundstrom sported even more muscle, but Josh looked furious. Then Sundstrom blanched. I'd never seen that before—a grown man with a tan actually turn white. It was something to see. So was two men—two big men—against one. The glances out to me told me not only were they fighting about me but also that I'd better get back to work. So, I did. I'd already seen enough, and I had better things to do, like concentrate on sculling. Once again, compartmentalization was my friend, and I'd become very adept at shoving things aside that had nothing to do with rowing. In two weeks, I would be competing against guys my age from all over the country.

In any event, the shit had not finished hitting the fan when I got off the water, not by a long shot. As I carried my single back to the boathouse, I saw Lodestone talking to a cop. Coach Sundstrom paced nearby, looking like he was about to dismember someone. The sudden weight in my stomach told me all I needed to know. I did not even need to see them glance over to me. Real subtle, guys. How about playing me a fanfare while you're at it?

As I went back down to the dock to pick up my oars, Jack pulled me aside. "Dude, what's going on?"

"I have no idea," I said wearily.

Jack shook his head. "You didn't do anything weird?"

"Life is getting baroque, but last I heard that wasn't a crime, so no." I tried to think what might have gone down while I was sculling but couldn't think of anything. Yet two of the Cap City coaches had practically mauled my not-boyfriend on the dock, and now there was a police officer waiting for me. Cops automatically made me worry. Damn, had they figured out what I had been doing all summer? I mean, I'd lied on two hookup sites... Shit. Maybe they would still let me row at the Youth Nationals.

"Leave him alone," Cisco said. "We've got our own equipment to deal with."

Cisco shot me a sympathetic look as he went back down to the dock to get their own oars while Jack trudged into the eights house where the pairs were stashed so he could wipe the water off their boat.

Meanwhile, I was alone in the singles house wiping down my boat when Lodestone, Sundstrom, and the cop cornered me. Maybe not intentionally, but when they got between me and the exit, they might as well have. I swallowed the lump in my throat.

"I am so sorry," Coach Sundstrom said, "Remy, is it? I had no idea Brennan would ever do something like that, or we never would've taken him on as an intern. When Nick finds out about this, he's going to kill the guy with his bare hands." The cop coughed. "Sorry, Officer. That's just a figure of speech."

"Understood," he said with a slight smile. "Actually, Mr. Babcock, I just wanted to talk—"

I frowned, although what I really wanted to do was puke. "Am I under arrest?"

"Oh no! Of course not, Remy! I just need to talk to you about Mr. Brennan and your relationship with him." The cop looked very embarrassed, and suddenly I knew the feeling. "I want to re-emphasize that you're not in any trouble and that you haven't done anything wrong, but I need some basic information and a detective down at the station will need to ask you some more questions, but that's all."

"Oh, okay, but I have to warn you, I've been out there sweating for a couple of hours and I don't smell very good." But if I wasn't under arrest, why was it three against one?

"I can get you into the CalPac boathouse," Lodestone said. "They have showers in their locker room. Will that be all right, Officer? Because he's right, sweaty rower is a unique smell you're probably not ready for."

The cop nodded reluctantly. "If it doesn't take too long."

"He'll be quick, and Remy? Expect an e-mail from me later, because I need to talk to you, as well." I calmed fractionally, but if I weren't in any trouble, why did Lodestone look like he wanted to murder me?

*

The uniformed officer had been correct. He had asked only basic questions, like my age and where I went to school. He skirted around the edges of my sexual orientation, but we both knew the answer to that. As it turned out, he had saved the hardball questions for Detective Jeanette Nakimoto.

"Thank you for coming in this afternoon," Detective Nakimoto said as she sat down in the interview room I had been cooling my jets in for the better part of an hour, an hour I had spent conjuring one nightmare scenario after another, each worse than the one before.

At least I'd had the chance to clean up, rehydrate, and eat, otherwise I would have been a lot less cooperative. Who knew, maybe the officer and the detective knew that. "I didn't think I had much choice."

Nakimoto sighed. "I'm sorry if we gave you that impression, but the reality is that we need your help if this case is going to stick."

"Really? Then the only way you're going to get that help is if you leave my parents out of this. I'm not out to them." I already did not like the direction this was heading, and if the good detective forced me to come all the way out, then she would find out just how uncooperative I could be. And I still felt like puking.

"I see," Nakimoto said.

"Do you? So far, I've been put on the spot in front of my teammates, and rowers gossip worse than old women, so this will be all over my rowing club by tonight, if it isn't already. My coach seems like he's ready to kill me, and someone I've been involved with has not only humiliated me publicly but has also been dragged off in chains," I said, trying to stop the wavering in my voice. "On top of it all, I've got a major competition in two weeks, and all of this is nothing but a distraction, a distraction I don't need. So why don't you go ahead and tell me why I should cooperate?"

Detective Nakimoto said nothing for a few moments. She only watched me long enough to make me squirm. "Okay, it was never our intention to make things bad for you. We were responding to a report of a potential crime of a sexual nature against a minor, and for that I can't and won't apologize, but I can see now that we should've handled it differently."

"You think?" I sniffled, but only because the air conditioning was so cold. At least, that was what I told myself. But "crime of a sexual nature against a minor"? Holy—damn. That sounded horrible, so predatory, like I had been a victim. I hadn't felt like a victim, not even when I'd seen the hickeys. I'd been angry and hurt, even humiliated, but not victimized.

"As to your request, for now, yes, I won't involve your parents as long as you help us," the detective said, "but I have to warn you that if this comes down to a criminal trial, you will be called as a witness whether you like it or not, and then yes, your parents will find out. I'm sorry, but it's the way these things work. I can make one promise—you'll have a lot of warning."

I bit my lip, thinking. Or I tried to think, anyway. This was...yeah. I barely remembered driving to the police station, and she wanted information. No wonder people demanded lawyers.

I eventually nodded. "Warning. I can work with that. So, what do you want to know?"

"Well, I have your answers to the officer's questions, and thank you for those," she said. "I have questions of my own, and some of them will seem redundant. At this point, I'm only trying to find out if a crime was even committed. California's laws about statutory rape can be a little peculiar."

Rape? "Whoa, Josh never raped me. Let's get that out there right now."

"*Statutory* rape," the detective said. "There's a big difference, and it's because you're still a minor and by legal definitions cannot consent to certain things. As I said, the law is a little murky at times. For instance, if two minors had consensual relations, by definition, they could both be guilty of unlawful sex."

I stared at her. "That's ridiculous."

"Of course, it is, but that's the way the law is written. So, it's vitally important to establish your age at the time you and Mr. Brennan started your relationship. Exactly how old were you?"

"A bit past my seventeenth birthday."

She looked at me intently. "You're sure? You're not rounding up?"

"I'm quite sure. He first met me when I was sixteen, and that's when he gave me his phone number, but I didn't call him until after I'd turned seventeen."

"That's interesting and useful to know." She made notes on a pad of paper for several minutes before she looked up at me again. "You contacted him, you said?"

I nodded. "Yeah." I felt the color rise in my cheeks, and not for the first time wished I could have another—any other—physical trait. "I was too chicken to do it any sooner."

"For what it's worth, that may make the difference between a misdemeanor and a felony, along with a lifetime on the sex offender registry," she said. "Another thing, Jeremy—do you prefer Jeremy or Remy?"

"Remy's fine, but thanks for asking."

"Another thing, Remy. Listen to your gut. It'll actually save you no end of trouble in life. People train themselves out of it but try to learn to listen to your instincts. That's what they're for. Anyway, so this was a consensual relationship?"

"It wasn't a relationship like we were boyfriends or anything. We were just using each other for sex." Hearing myself say it out loud like that? It sounded sad, even pathetic.

"All right," Nakimoto said as she made more notes. "Do you think he knew you were a minor when you met? When you hooked up?"

"Actually, I highly doubt he knew," I admitted. "I certainly didn't volunteer the information." I paused. "The thing is, Detective? My brother and I, we're fraternal twins by the way, we've always looked older than our age. We were first asked what we were majoring in when we were in the ninth grade or so. So, the first time Josh met me? Despite the fact the boatyard was full of people who were obviously teenagers, I was off doing my own thing, and he probably thought I was an assistant coach or something."

She frowned at me. "Would you mind standing up for me?"

I squirmed a bit as she examined me. I was tempted to ask if she wanted to check my hooves and teeth but managed to keep my mouth shut. I wasn't in any trouble, and I wanted it to stay that way.

"You're right. If I didn't know your age, I wouldn't peg you for a high schooler."

I wasn't lying.

Thank you very much for taking me seriously, cop lady.

She waved for me to sit back down. "Well, Remy, this is certainly much more complicated than it first appeared."

Duh. "So, what's going to happen to him?"

"Do you care about him?"

I shook my head. "No, not really. He was convenient. Do you want to know what started your involvement off?"

"Yes, as a matter of fact," Nakimoto said.

"I'll bet." I snorted. "He showed up at the boathouse with so many hickeys he looked like he'd been attacked by a vacuum cleaner. Mind you, we weren't dating or anything exclusive like that, but I'm not altogether out, and I'd thought we owed each other a certain amount of discretion."

"That seems reasonable."

"I guess I was the only one who thought that, and I'm apparently not as good as I thought about keeping things like that off my face. Either that or my coach—"

"This would be Peter Lodestone?"

"Right, so either I'm lousy at keeping my feelings off my face or Lodestone's better at reading me than I thought, because the next thing I knew, he had figured it all out and was in the middle of a fight with Josh and then dragged Coach Sundstrom into it."

Detective Nakimoto looked at me for long moments. "You're young yet. Not being able to mask your feelings isn't necessarily a failing."

"Seemed like it this morning," I muttered.

"I know. Give it time and you'll be every bit as jaded as the rest of us." She sounded far wearier than she had moments before. "Anyway, this Coach Sundstrom, he would be Mr. Brennan's supervisor in adaptive rowing?"

"I guess," I sighed. "Yes."

"Tell me about adaptive rowing. You assisted with it as your summer job."

I nodded. "It's a way to get people who lack full mobility into boats. You know, exercise what they've got by modifying the boats to suit them, usually in a two-person boat with an able-bodied rower. I was the able-bodied rower, obviously. It's pretty cool if you think about it."

"It is indeed." She checked over her notes like she wanted to be sure she had not missed anything important. "I know this will be uncomfortable for you, but I need more information and detail than 'hooking up.'"

I stared at the detective. "You're kidding."

"No, I'm afraid not. The law is very specific. I need to know what acts you and Mr. Brennan did and how often. It'll help make the determination between misdemeanor and felony, although a lot of that depends on the age spread, frankly." It did not make me feel any better that she seemed embarrassed too.

I felt myself heating up. "Is there any way I can write this down? Because I'm pretty sure telling you all this would make me die of mortification."

Detective Nakimoto slid another pad of paper and a pen across the table to me. "I'll be at the other end of the table with my laptop. I've got things I can work on while you write me a narrative of your summer with Mr. Brennan, starting with how you met and how you hooked up the first time. Something tells me this is important."

And that was how I passed the most excruciating thirty minutes of my life. She wanted it all, and that was what I gave her, at least so far as Josh and I were concerned. The rest of my extracurricular activities this summer were exactly that—mine. She didn't need to know about my adventures with hookup apps. However, the fact that this was a criminal investigation had slowly started to pierce my standard rowing-related obliviousness. It scared me, and I had two major fears: that somehow it would keep me from competing in the Youth Nationals and that the good detective would find a reason to tell my parents. I needed to do what the police wanted.

When I finished, I coughed to get her attention. "I'm sorry to bother you, but is this all right? I'm afraid I can't remember every single thing, and honestly, it's probably not as much as you're thinking it was."

Detective Nakimoto scanned what I had written down. "I think I have what I need for now, although I will doubtless be in touch with you. I'll call your cell phone to protect your privacy. I won't use e-mail because that's not secure."

"So, what happens next?" That was the big question and the one that scared me the most.

She looked at me with sympathy. "For you? You do your best to put this out of your mind and concentrate on that national competition coming up. The wheels of justice turn slowly, particularly with the courts being so overburdened. For me, I'll continue to interview people and gather evidence to see if there's enough to send this to the district attorney. It's up to him to make the call about whether or not there's a case here."

"Do you think there is? If you had to guess and off the record and all that?" I said.

"That's a tough question and one of the reasons I'm glad I'm not the DA." Detective Nakimoto thought about it. She looked like she gave it her honest consideration and didn't just blow me off. "I'll say this much. The law states that he could be guilty of either a misdemeanor or a felony, depending on his criminal history. The fact that you two are so close in age means he falls within the window of discretion between the two classes of criminal act. That you sought him out and hid your age could count as a mitigating factor. The ball's in his court, and I haven't interviewed him yet. I'm sorry if this sounds like a cop-out, but right now it's all I've got."

"I understand. Are there any more questions, or can I go?"

The detective looked at the time. "Will you be in trouble for being so late?"

"Only with my brother for hogging the car, but I texted him before we started, so he knew to take our shared Vespa to work," I said. "He told our parents I had to stay late for practice."

"You two are thick as thieves, aren't you?" When I started to stall, she continued, "Don't even bother. I'm a twin myself."

I nodded. "I'd be lost without him."

Chapter Nine

Sure enough, when I checked my e-mail on my phone in the parking lot of the West Sacramento PD, I found a terse e-mail from Lodestone. Somehow, I knew that my interrogation by the detective had been nothing compared to the one I faced at the hands of my coach.

I made it home in time to hand the car off to Goff after all, decreasing by one my list of things to feel guilty about. I also managed to beat both Mom and Dad home, decreasing by one the number of things I had to lie about. Since I had dinner about halfway done by the time both parents made it home and also helped clean up, no one had any issue with me meeting Lodestone to "discuss race strategy" after dinner. I saw no point in putting this off.

I had wanted to meet in a public place, because duh, I'm not stupid and I knew that whatever Lodestone had in store for me would not be pleasant, but my coach prevailed.

"Walk with me, Remy," Lodestone said. So, we picked up warm beverages at Peet's downtown to ward off the chill of a summer evening in the Sacramento Valley and then went for a walk away from the city center toward Central Park.

"So, what's going on, Remy? What the hell was today about?" Lodestone said.

I squirmed in the darkness. "It's really kind of personal."

"Oh, for the love of—that's not good enough, not this time. I had to call the police on the adaptive program's intern for statutory rape, Remy."

That tore it. "You know, Coach, it *is* personal, and it'll *have* to be good enough, because it's none of your business." He didn't say anything for a few moments, and I hardly knew what to make of that, but my temper kept ratcheting up.

"Remy—Jeremy—when another coach preys on one of my rowers, it actually *is* my business. I absolutely *cannot* have a sexual predator anywhere near my program." I could tell Lodestone fought manfully to keep his temper under control, but he wasn't the only one with a temper.

Why the hell did everyone see this as predatory? I totally understood that the age differences weren't necessarily cool. A twenty-year-old and someone younger than me? Yuck, and get the shotgun and the pruning shears. Or someone older than Josh going after me? Oh hell no. I would have called the cops myself. But there was nothing special about my eighteenth birthday. I would not magically discover sex that day, and there was no use pretending otherwise. I understood why those laws existed. I truly did. There were people too young to consent, and if mental age were taken into account, some people would never be old enough. I, however, could consent and had, but no one would listen to me.

"You should've asked me first, Coach. You should have fucking asked." I felt my voice thickening with rage. Then something horrible occurred to me, something that rocked my world on its axis. "Is this some kind of gay thing?"

Lodestone spun me around so fast I dropped my tea. "No, and you listen and you listen good, kiddo. Don't you dare play the homophobia card with me. This has nothing to do with homophobia and everything to do with stopping a sexual predator."

"Sexual predator?" I laughed, but my voice verged on the hysteric. "Are you kidding me? I went after him."

"That's what he said, but I don't believe it, not entirely, and it really doesn't matter."

I sputtered. "It doesn't matter? How the hell can it not matter?"

"I'm not a lawyer, but it depends on how much older than you he is." Lodestone looked at me. "Well? How much older is he?"

"I don't know, but the detective said the same thing."

Lodestone sighed. "I think you'd better find out."

"I really don't see why you're making such a big deal about this. I was upset this morning, yes, but that was between Josh and me. I'm sorry other people are involved, but it won't happen again." If only because after my talk with Detective Nakimoto, I knew that Josh would never speak to me again, not that I wanted him to. Honestly, what more did Lodestone want me to say?

Lodestone's jaw clenched. I didn't think I'd ever seen him so angry. "It's not just you and your closet on the line here, Remy. It's me and my future as a coach. It's the juniors rowing program. Hell, it's all of Cap City. Josh was working with the adaptive rowing program, so it's Coach Sundstrom, it's Coach Bedford. It's all of us and everything everyone associated with Cap City has worked for. I get that teens can be self-centered naturally, but you really need to work your way around that, because honestly? You're being a selfish asshole, and I don't like you very much right now."

"What? How?" That was just too much. I gave Lodestone and crew everything. I had no social life, my grades were lower than they would have been, people mocked me for my single-minded obsession with the sport, but it was all worth it because everything I gave crew, I received back tenfold. Or thought I did.

"If I didn't report this, I'd be in legal jeopardy as an accessory to statutory rape." Lodestone sounded like he was explaining this to a child, and a particularly stupid one at that.

He sounded just like the detective, and I told him what I told her. "Rape? He never raped me."

"Statutory rape. There's a difference, and you'd better learn the difference. It's when someone too young to give legal consent has sex with someone old enough to know better. From what the police told me, the law's a little different in California. It all depends on your relative ages. This all might blow over in a week, or you could be looking at a drawn-out legal mess. Do your parents even know?"

My mouth hung open. He wouldn't dare.

"I see I've finally gotten your attention." Lodestone shook his head. "Think, Remy. You're an intelligent young man, but you're completely self-absorbed. Until recently, I'd thought your total focus on rowing was an asset, even a gift, but now I have to question that. You need to step back and look around. There's a lot more to your life than rowing."

But there wasn't, not since Mikey had thrown me out of his bedroom. I realized that now. I had thrown myself into crew—and that other thing—to avoid thinking about Mikey. As far as realizations went, that one sucked, and I pulled away from it like it burned. *Hic sunt dracones* and all that.

"What...what about practice? The Youth Nationals are in two weeks."

Lodestone laughed, but I didn't think there was any humor in it. "You're something else, Remy. I don't know whether to tie you up and deliver you to your parents with instructions that you never set foot in my boathouse again or applaud your determination to win, I really don't. Yes, you have practice as usual."

"Then that's all that really matters." I turned and left. I wouldn't give him a chance to see me crack, not after what he had just told me. He had been my mentor, my hero, but now? I didn't know anything anymore. That was not true, strictly speaking. I still had rowing, even if Lodestone himself had broken faith. People might come and go, but my devotion to crew would never and could never waver. The water would always be there for me, the water and the ergometer. People could play me false, but those two would reward my devotion. They always had before.

"Remy!" I heard Lodestone call, but I ignored him. He was not one of my favorite people at that moment. I knew I would have to think about his words later, but just then I was homesick for anywhere but there.

I took off, running back to where I'd parked the Vespa.

*

I fired off an irate text as soon as I got home.

> REMY: *Men are dicks, all of them—alleged best friends, hookups, coaches, all of them are dicks.*

It didn't take long for my friend Todd to text back. He had chatted me up on Grindr one day early in the summer, apparently able to tell from my pictures that I rowed. He himself had rowed in high school and now rowed as a freshman in college and was an assistant coach for a juniors program to earn money. It had not taken very long before we'd abandoned innuendo-laden flirting for crew babble. Okay, we still flirted once in a while, but mostly we kept it under control. Todd was an interesting soul, and if we had lived closer to one another, we might have hooked up. As it was, we settled for a long-distance friendship. We were only a year apart in age—he was eighteen to my seventeen—and that made it very easy to talk to him. That said, I knew where that tall blond stud had some interesting tattoos.

TODD: *Well, duh. What brought about this revelation, pray tell?*

REMY: *How long have U got?*

TODD: *About 8 inches.*

REMY: *Don't make me kill you.*

TODD: *Sorry, go ahead.*

So, I did. I unloaded all over him.

TODD: *So what's wrong with slowing down?*

I blinked. He was right.

REMY: *Not a damn thing.*

TODD: *Oh hey, guess what? I didn't tell U sooner cuz it wasn't a sure thing but guess who's coming to Youth Nat'ls?*

So, I slowed down. I flat-out ignored Adams2Steves.com and deleted Grindr from my phone.

They were distractions, and I needed to process everything that had happened vis-à-vis Josh, although I had a sneaking suspicion that might take a good long time. You picked up a thing or two when one of your parents was a shrink, and I did not mean spare neuroses. If my gut told me I needed to process, then that was what I needed. Funny how my gut had already started to sound like Detective Nakimoto, but the thing was, she was right. We do train ourselves not to listen to our guts, which is nothing more than a crude term for instincts. Some people say humans don't have instincts, but I don't think that's true. What we have are the critical faculties to convince ourselves there are no things that go bump in the night and there aren't monsters in the skins of men. When I wasn't sculling, I went back over every single encounter I had ever had with Josh.

Then there was that staggering realization I had stumbled over about how I had spent my summer after Mikey's rejection. Early in the summer, Mikey told me the first time that he was waiting for the right guy and the right time, so I buried my hurt fee-fees and called Josh. After we'd done our thing, Josh and I, I ended up calling Mikey anyway because even still, he had been my best friend. Looking back, Mikey had been by turns fascinated and repelled by what I told him. And weirdly hung up on my T-shirt. He reiterated his stance on the right guy and the right time, and that twisted like a knife in my heart since it reminded me I wasn't it. Then he kicked me out. That was the moment—the exact moment—when I turned into a cockhound.

Looking back, that had clearly been the wrong thing to do, because Lodestone called the cops on Josh when things went sour. Was it weird that part of me thought Josh and I could've salvaged things if only people could've left us the hell alone? Scream and yell, make-up sex, and then it would've been fine. Or not. It still would've been ours to end. Jeez, could I even hear my own thoughts? Monsters in the skins of men? Maybe I wanted to have been the one to pull the plug?

Besides which, if there were any truth at all to my realization about Mikey's rejection and how I spent my summer, not only should I have ignored those hookup sites, I should have deleted them immediately. Oh well, better to realize it late than never. There was a saying about that, one I thought I remembered from freshman-year humanities. Minerva's owl flies at dusk? Great, more classicism from the mouths of babes. I had to get out of this town.

Oh, Mikey and my T-shirts. I automatically glanced at the one I was wearing. I'd chosen it to piss off Lodestone, actually. "I'm not gay, but $20 is $20." Goff almost choked on his cereal when he saw it at breakfast. It was a little tight, but not too much worse than the others. Whatever. Come to think of it, Mikey was at the boathouse this morning, and when he saw it, he dropped his duffel bag and stood there with his mouth open. I'd gotten so used to ignoring him that it barely registered.

*

Since the men's and women's crews combined entered fewer crews for the Nationals than the Crew Classic, de-rigging and loading the trailer struck me as lower key. I don't think I was alone.

"He won't be here, if that's who you're looking for," Lodestone said quietly when he noticed me looking around.

I hadn't realized I was, but the circumstances were much the same as they had been for the Crew Classic once I thought about it. I was de-rigging a small boat, in this case the single I planned to race. Cisco and Jack worked nearby on the pair they'd be racing.

"Good." I felt Lodestone's eyes still on me, but I didn't say anything.

"Remy...if there's anything you want to..."

I looked up. "No."

What did he want me to say? Gosh, Coach, Josh and I have been getting it on all summer, and we still would be, but I screwed it up by overreacting to his hickeys. If he hadn't been mauled or I'd been better at hiding my disappointment, you'd never have known about this and called the cops.

He looked like he didn't believe me. His choice. I had a boat to de-rig. I tried to smile. I'm sure it came out looking like I was about to bite him. Smiles never came naturally to me. Why did so much of my life lately consist of reassuring adults of my mental status?

I finished with my single and all its parts. "You guys need any help?"

Jack nodded. "We wouldn't turn it down."

"Can you bind up the riggers?" Cisco said.

"I'm on it." The ritual of the process calmed me in a way. We'd all done our best to prepare. The races started the day after tomorrow, and we were into our taper. Sure, we'd have short, hard rows at the venue, but the long practices were done. Now all that was left was for me to psych myself out, but the common chores like these kept me from that. I suspected Lodestone had me figured out by now, which was why he inevitably assigned me to de-rig and re-rig. Then, too, as soon as I reached the venue, I'd take my prerace walk to suss out the course, never mind how many times I'd raced on it.

After we had secured all the rowing shells to the trailer and stowed the rigging and boxes of spare parts in the base of said trailer, we were essentially done.

"All right, ladies and gentlemen, this is it. You've worked hard all year and especially all summer for this," Lodestone said. He had been the coach in charge because he had been able to take the afternoon off. Sabrina Littlewolf was at work, as nurses were in demand and she had been required to work overtime. "I want you to take it easy for the rest of the afternoon and get a good night's rest. Sleep in tomorrow morning and tell your parents it's coach's orders."

We all laughed at that. Our parents knew the score and had agreed to this when they had given permission for us to participate in the Nationals.

"I'll be driving the trailer up to Lake Natoma in the morning, and I expect to see you all—rested—by noon," Lodestone continued. "Any questions?"

Someone from the girls' team raised her hand. "How much do we need to bring in the way of food or drinks or anything?"

I stifled my groan. She had been rowing with the junior crew as long as I had. Had we *ever* had to bring anything? I mean, there was a reason the juniors' program cost so much.

"Don't worry about a thing, unless there's something special you want or need. At this point, it's about race psychology. There'll be the usual parent volunteer table there," Lodestone said. "If you want a T-shirt or any other merchandise to validate the experience, you'll need money, otherwise, that's it. Anything else?"

When no one said anything, Lodestone said, "Git, y'all."

"Git, y'all?" I said as everyone left.

Lodestone smiled. "I've told you guys about how French is the international language for crew, right?"

"It's called *aviron* in French, right?"

Lodestone nodded. I used to love these times when it was just the two of us. He always seemed more relaxed, even freer somehow, but now? Would I ever recapture that? "Right, so the command to start a race used to be in French—*à vos marques, prêts, partez!* I've never actually heard that at a regatta, by the way, only during practice in college. Well, one time in college, I was at a regatta in

Texas, and I swear, the starter forgot it was a USRowing event or something and yelled, 'Git, y'all!' Funniest thing I've ever heard."

Regattas had always seemed so constipated, with an air of High Seriousness. The thought of an actual USRowing official saying this had me doubled over in seconds. "That... Oh my gawd."

"Easy there, sport," Lodestone said as I struggled to regain my breath. He still had a smile on his face though.

"You realize that's all I'll hear tomorrow, right?"

He nudged me with his elbow. "That might've been why I said it. You tend to wind yourself up."

I longed to nudge him back but could not bring myself to do it. "Maybe just a bit."

"I'll see you tomorrow, Remy. Have a good night."

"Good evening, Coach Lodestone."

Behind me, I knew he was frowning but couldn't bring myself to care.

Chapter Ten

I woke up at a leisurely pace in the morning. My parents had already left for work. They had offered to come see me race, but I hadn't thought it necessary. They had seen me race before, after all, and I had plans up there that definitely did not include them. They weren't offended, and we planned to go out to dinner that evening when I intended to have hardware—medals—around my neck.

Goff was still home, however, since he had changed his work schedule after the SAT prep and summer school had ended. He knocked on my bedroom door.

"Yeah?"

He stuck his head in and was all smiles. "Hey, you're awake. I just wanted to wish you luck before I left for work. You sure you don't need anyone up there to cheer you on?"

"I'm fine." I smiled back. "It feels like a good day to race."

"Is the only pace suicide pace?" he asked, the old crew joke.

I nodded. "And it's a good day to die."

"You're insane." He shook his head. This from a man who regularly let people the size of major appliances land on him?

"I'd be the last to know, I guess."

"Text me the results, okay?"

I smiled again. "Absolutely."

"Okay, I gotta go. See you tonight." Goff ducked out and left.

I didn't bother to shower. What was the point? In a few hours I'd be sweating like a thoroughbred.

Then I got a text, hopefully from Todd, my tatted Viking. I think I had a crush on him just from texting. How pitiful was that? Or maybe I was just pitiful.

I dove for my phone. Yep, pitiful.

TODD: *See U in a few hours, buddy*

REMY: *It'll B good 2 finally meet in person.*

TODD: *Team colors?*

REMY: *Here's a pic of me in my uni.*

TODD: *Daaaamn.*

REMY: *Stop it. Now my uni doesn't fit right.*

TODD: *Picture. Now.*

I shivered and complied, even though he had changed the terms of our relationship. Or maybe this had been there from the beginning, waiting. Regardless, I was coming to realize I liked being told what to do.

I quickly received one in return.

TODD: *U do this 2 me.*

He was rock hard.

REMY: *You'll find me?*

TODD: *Bet on it and not just because UR hot, Remy. I want to meet U IRL 2.*

I smiled.

REMY: *Me 2. Now I've gotta get busy or I'll B late.*

TODD: *Don't U dare :-)*

I had my orders, didn't I?

*

The Cap City junior crew got lucky this year. The USRowing Youth Nationals were held at Lake Natoma, just east of Sacramento, forty-five minutes away from our boathouse. That was as the boat-trailer drove, not as normal traffic moved. As far as regattas went, it was in our backyard. Last year it had been in Oak Ridge, TN, and talk about an expensive trip. We'd spent as much time raising money for the trip as practicing. Anyway, all the rowing clubs and programs in Northern California, if not the northern Pacific coast, lucked out in another way. The course at Lake Natoma on the American River counted as one of the best in North America. That the dam operators were willing to oblige regatta organizers by raising or lowering the water level made it all the better. Okay, the river lacked docks, which entailed wading out into the water, just like the Crew Classic. Since runoff from the Sierra snowpack fed the river, fall races with their colder weather could be an exercise in misery, but in late July? It was heaven.

As always at a regatta, re-rigging was the first order of business. We carried all the boats from the trailer to the staging area along with their rigging and the equipment boxes. Who would row what didn't matter; men and women carried each other's boats. What mattered was transporting boats from the trailer to the slings waiting in our assigned place along the beach.

I worked on my single, but I felt Mikey glaring at me the entire time. I didn't even know what I'd done this time. Probably nothing. Every time I looked up at him, he'd look away quickly, but I knew what that game looked like. What I couldn't figure out was why he was there in the first place. He wasn't rowing in the regatta and kissing the coach's ass was not a part of his makeup, particularly since Lodestone wasn't even his coach.

Another thing puzzled me, however. Where was Cisco?

I wasn't the only one who missed him.

"Where's my pair partner? I'm going to have a hard time racing if he doesn't show up," Jack said. He had a point.

"We've got time," Lodestone said.

That didn't stop our coach from checking his watch with increasing frequency. I also noticed that he called Cisco more than once. As much as being late to a regatta was not done, things happened. Maybe traffic had gotten bad after I'd arrived at Lake Natoma. It wouldn't have been the first time. Or his car had trouble. Things happened. Not calling, however? That was unusual. Cisco was a stand-up guy.

I put it out of my mind. Jack and Lodestone were worrying enough for the whole team, and ultimately it would have no impact on my race. I needed to get moving if I was going to walk the course before my practice row.

"Walking?" Jack said.

I nodded. "You know it."

"Can I come with?"

"Always." I'd hoped to go find Todd, but what could I have said?

"Hey, Mikey! You coming?" Jack called.

I flinched. Great. The whole team, even the women, were joining me. Oh well, nothing to be done about it, especially not since Goody Castelreigh, who seemed to be in a censorious mood again, decided to tag along. So much for scoping out Todd on the sly.

The Nationals course was the same length as the Crew Classic—two thousand meters—but unlike that race, I only went through the motions. I'd rowed this course so many times, and I was so distracted, but unlike the San Diego race, the weather up here was far less variable. Yet there I was, walking the two thousand meters again, pretending to look at the water levels and where in the river the regatta organizers had situated the race lanes, things like that. It struck me as so pointless. The race would be what it was, and I'd verify it empirically all too soon.

And there he was, my tatted Viking. Todd kept it strictly professional. His program—the one he coached for, not the one he rowed for—had fielded a much larger crew than Cap City, which explained why he was there as assistant coach. Funny, that. They had had to travel much farther than we did, but perhaps it was a larger club or maybe they were just better than we were this year. But that wasn't what I was thinking about right then. He stayed in coaching mode, I stayed in rower mode, just another high school rower amidst his teammates. But eye contact was established, and I saw a definite glint in his eye. He turned away as quickly as he'd made eye contact, but a short time later my phone vibrated in my pocket.

I played it cool. I didn't check the message until we were back to Cap City's boats. I had to work hard to keep my face neutral as I read his message: very precise instructions on where to meet him after my row. He even included a picture of the location. Fortunately, I knew this venue well.

I opened a sports drink, but drank only a small amount, mostly to stay hydrated rather than tank up. It was time for a practice row, anyhow. "Any instructions, Coach?"

"I want you on the water for no more than a half hour. That includes warming up and cooling for ten minutes each. That leaves you ten minutes for hard work," Lodestone said. "This is just to warm your muscles up and keep them warm, and nothing more. That goes for all of you. Ladies, you too, unless Coach Littlewolf has told you something different. These prerace practices aren't to increase your conditioning. You're in the shape you're going to be in..."

I nodded obediently. I knew all this. He said it before every race. I had other things on my mind, things like Todd. Something had shifted, maybe with this morning's texting, maybe with the knowledge that we'd be in the same general area. We weren't flirting anymore, we were circling, sniffing each other out. Now that I knew what to look for, I realized I could see Todd clearly from where we were. He could see me too. I felt his eyes on me while I stripped down to my uni. Smiling to myself, I stretched and scratched. I couldn't hear him, but I certainly saw him stumble.

"Crap!"

I looked up. Mikey had spilled chocolate milk down his front and was now glaring at me, like somehow it was my fault. I would never understand him, but then, it wasn't my job to either. I realized that by launching and taking a practice row I could escape Mikey and his issues.

"Mikey?" I heard Lodestone say. "There's still no sign of Cisco. If he's not here in fifteen minutes, could you go out with Jack? I'd like him to get a row in too..."

I frowned. It really wasn't like Cisco to be so late for a regatta.

*

I'd taken my practice row and then found some shade to rest in. Fortunately, a breeze took the edge off the heat, enough to cool the place off but not so much as to count as a crosswind. Crosswinds bad, cooling off in late July good. Watching the races might have been courteous, but I launched in a few minutes as it was, and I wanted to rest up and psych myself up.

I sensed rather than saw someone sit next to me. "Hi," Mikey said softly.

"Hey."

The silence thickened.

"You're not going to make this easy on me, are you?" He laughed uncomfortably.

I sighed. "I launch in less than ten minutes. It's a big race. I'm not in the mood for any drama, and Mikey? All I've gotten from you since school got out is drama."

"I know, and I'm sorry. That's...that's what I wanted to talk about," he said, his voice almost too quiet to hear.

I sat up and looked at him. That was the last thing I needed right then. "Did you hear me? This needs to wait. You've waited this long. Another hour won't kill you."

"You know what? Never mind." Mikey got up. "Forget I said anything."

Fat chance. "Thanks, Mikey. Timing's everything, and yours sucks."

I tried to ignore him as he stomped off. I abandoned any hope of real rest and tried to focus on deep breathing to calm down, but it was a lost cause. I gave it up and got ready to launch. More sunscreen, oars to the water, and then Lodestone.

When I reached Lodestone, he was on his phone. "Cisco, man. Where are you? Call me."

I frowned, worried now. This was so unlike Cisco.

"Anything to say before I launch?"

Lodestone shook his head. "This is your race to lose. The competition will be stiff, but you know that. Keep your head in your boat and in your lane. When you get excited, you sometimes row at a higher rating than you need to, so don't be afraid to take your pace down a few strokes per minute."

I nodded. "Right-o. Time to get on the water."

Whatever my distractions on land—I saw Todd wink at me as I took my single to the water but ignored him—I focused on the water and the rowing to the exclusion of all else. It irritated my friends, or so I was told, but they weren't the ones rowing in the Youth Nationals.

Carrying my boat on one shoulder, I waded out until the water lapped at the bottom of my unisuit. Flipping it up and overhead, I placed my boat in the water and held it steady while someone brought me my oars. I've seen some scullers who could do it all, but I wasn't there, yet.

By the time I had the oars secured in the oarlocks I was so deep inside my rowing headspace I didn't even know who had helped me. Then I climbed into my boat. I could have done this in my sleep, but I was wide awake and taking everything in as I paddled away from the shore.

The American River just before the Nimbus Dam was wide enough to accommodate six lanes this year. I had seen seven after particularly wet winters. It all depended on how much runoff came down from the Sierra Nevada range, or rather, on how much water the dam operators thought they could spare if they fiddled with the water levels for us. Oddly enough, regattas weren't the reason the dam existed.

I had an okay lane, not great. I was on the far side of the course but not the farthest lane. Those far lanes usually felt the crosswinds the worst, but it was a poor rower who blamed his performance on weather, at least not until the weather turned severe. Chop, strong winds, hail, lightning, sure, but this little breeze? I ignored it in favor of getting to my lane before the line refs grew cranky. So long as I wasn't the last one at the line, I was golden.

I sized up my competition. I was larger than a lot of the other scullers, save for one guy. He looked like a gorilla. On the one hand, more muscle mass meant more weight to haul down the course. On the other, the water supported a lot of that weight. Still, I pegged him as the one to watch. I could just see him out of the corner of my eyes. Sure, being on the starting line like that was always a head trip, but I also knew that they all felt the same way and at least one of the guys was no doubt thinking the same thing about me. I smiled and sat confidently in my start position. Let them sweat. I was ready.

"We have alignment," the announcer said.

"Ready all!"

The muscles of my legs bunched, coiling like powerful springs, ready to push the boat from a dead stop into motion with the first stroke.

"Row!"

Git, y'all!

I laughed as I left the line.

The thing was, even with a single, I couldn't just go from a dead stop to full speed. Doing so only courted premature exhaustion and risked injury. So, I used a fairly common start sequence. A first stroke that was legs-only—no back swing and no arms—and only half of the slide, just enough to overcome the boat's inertia, and then two more quick strokes that used only three-quarters of the slide and nothing else, and then a final legs-only stroke before lengthening a bit and taking "twenty high," twenty strokes above my planned pace for the rest of the race. That was what Lodestone had meant about rowing too fast. I had the nasty habit of lengthening my stroke out—legs, body swing, and arms—while still maintaining a high number of strokes per minute.

It drove Lodestone crazy when he was coaching me, particularly when other people were trying to follow me, but out here? I was alone. Races had been lost because some fool turned his head to look around—no joke—but I could flick my eyes back and forth. But that afternoon, I didn't need to. I counted five people behind me, which looked like in front of me. Join crew! Find happiness looking backward! That said, the gorilla and a smaller guy were gaining on me, and hell no.

The only pace is suicide pace, and today is a good day to die.

Up to this point, I'd been rowing at a fast clip, but my ratio—the speed of my leg drive down the tracks that held the seat compared to the time it took me to travel back up to get back into position for another stroke—needed improvement. That was one reason Lodestone distrusted my tendency to speed. If I kept the ratio clean, great. I flew across the top of the water. If I got sloppy, I wasted my energy and didn't let the mechanism of the boat do its job. I'd gotten sloppy, and the result was those two guys gaining on me.

With a deep breath and herculean effort, I marshaled all my focus and forced myself to slow down my recovery. "Let the boat run under you, Remy," I repeated over and over. A longer recovery meant more oxygen for my starved muscles, which in turn meant stronger leg drives.

Slowly, I pulled away from my competition, and by the fifteen-hundred-meter mark, my change had made a noticeable difference. Sure, the gorilla and the smaller guy made changes in response, but would it be enough to make a difference?

I'd wasted a lot of energy earlier in the race. I knew that, but with five hundred meters left, it was time to make a move. I didn't have much choice. My two challengers were making theirs, trying to outsprint me at the end because they knew the mistake I'd made too.

This was it. I had to empty the tank and hope I had enough left to last. Struggling to maintain that all-important ratio, I brought the stroke rating back up. At that point, technique was a fantasy. All I did was hack at the water.

By the time I saw the red buoys marking the final one hundred meters, the gorilla and I were bow to stern. If I let up for even a second, that ape would take the race. Son of a bitch. I was pissed. My race to lose, huh? We'd just see about that.

It was personal now. The gorilla knew it and I knew it. He looked over his shoulder and his boat wobbled. That was it. My legs burned with all the fires of hell, but I stood on the foot stretchers for the last ten strokes. I didn't care how I hurt or if I broke the boat. I was going to win this if it was the last thing I did or if I popped a tendon. This race was mine, dammit.

Then the air horn blared. I had won, but it had been close, hard-fought, and only by half a boat length. I was furious and had only myself to blame.

"Good row, man," Gorilla said.

I was pretty sure I managed something polite in return, but it was time for me to be out of there. Out of my headspace, I remembered Todd. What was going on with him? I knew he wanted to meet, but beyond that? I was bereft of clue and rowing back to shore was not the time to hunt for one. Far too many boats jockeyed for position for me to space out.

I paddled back to Cap City's stretch of beach, allowing myself a small smile as I passed Todd. To my surprise, he unabashedly stared as I passed. Maybe he was telling his rowers what not to do.

When I landed, far enough from the shore that I wouldn't scratch the rowing shell's hull, no one was there to take the oars. Classy. Someone was *always* supposed to be there to take the oars.

I didn't think the current would take the boat, so I took one oar out of its oarlock and anchored the other oar's handle in the sand, hoping it would hold long enough to dash up the beach and stash the first oar. I figured I could handle the boat and the other oar.

I guess Todd saw me struggling because he ran up to me. "What the hell? Where're your teammates?"

"Beats me." My mood had grown worse since I landed.

Todd looked at me. "You okay?"

"It was a shitty row, and this isn't helping."

"For what it's worth, you looked good out there," he said. Then he gave me a once-over, grinning slowly.

I laughed; I couldn't help it. "Thanks. I threw my race plan right out and then scrambled to make up for it during the second thousand meters. Then my team was apparently busy enough that a coach from another team has to come help me. Not that I'm not grateful, by the way. It's all just…"

"I get it." Todd moved in closer. "Just like I'm going to get you in about twenty. You still game?"

I shuddered and then checked my heart-rate monitor for the time. "Yes."

Todd had to hustle back to his own team, especially if he was going to disappear in twenty minutes, but he first helped me with the oars as I carried my boat back to its slings.

"Hey, thanks for the help, you guys!" I said brightly as I lowered the boat into the slings.

Some of them jumped, like they'd forgotten about me, and that felt oh so swell. At least a few looked guilty. Good. You're there when your teammates land. Period.

I sighed. What was the point? Suddenly none of it felt like it mattered. I was about to start on the de-rigging and then realized that didn't matter either. Someone else could do it. I had just worked rather hard, and I wanted to rest and stretch.

Instead I grabbed a sports drink and a protein shake from the parent volunteer table and started to stretch. The last thing I needed was a set of cramps due to dehydration or loss of electrolytes.

A shadow fell over me, and I looked up, expecting to see Mikey. It was Lodestone.

"No one met you, did they?" he said.

I didn't trust myself to say much, particularly not to him. "No."

"I'm really sorry."

"Whatever." I turned back to my stretching, unwilling to admit to him just how it had hurt, how betrayed I had felt at that moment. Maybe I hadn't wanted to admit it myself either. I'd always bought into the "team" bit wholeheartedly, but now... I wasn't so sure. "It's fine."

Lodestone sat down. "It's not, is it?"

I hated how well he could read me. Hated it. I jumped up. "Not now. Not right fucking now," I yelled.

I took off down the jogging path that snaked around Lake Natoma.

"Remy!" he called.

I ignored him.

At the end of it all, he wasn't the boss of me.

Chapter Eleven

I made it halfway around the lake before I remembered there was somewhere else I wanted to be. *Good going, Remy*, I thought. *You're cocking it up left and right today.*

I turned around, not at all sure I wanted to meet Todd anymore, not at all sure I *should* meet him just then. I mean, how much more of a buzz killer could the day turn out to be? But I found my way to the place Todd had suggested, an out-of-the-way spot, secluded and neglected. Hope there weren't any rattlers...

One thing for sure, with all the dried leaves and pine needles, we'd hear anyone approaching, which was how I knew Todd had arrived.

He stepped up behind me and embraced me from behind. I relaxed into him. It was actually a relief to do so. I realized something in that moment too. This was what I had been missing all summer, and I hadn't even known it.

Todd kissed the back of my neck, and I arched into it. "Hey, beautiful," he said.

"Hi."

"Is this okay?" he said.

I thought about it for the briefest moment because that was all it took. "Yes."

"Good, because do you have any idea how long I've been waiting to do this?"

I shook my head. "All day?"

"Since we first started getting to know each other."

I didn't know what to say to that. I pulled his arms tighter around me instead.

"Is something wrong?" he asked.

"Yes? No? Maybe?"

"Can you repeat the question?" He laughed. "What? I like They Might Be Giants too."

"Let's go sit down," I said, pointing at a picnic table, "but watch your feet. There're snakes up here, and some are poisonous."

Todd froze. "You're kidding."

"No, but rattlesnakes almost always warn you before they strike." I tugged on his hand, finally getting him moving.

I ended up spilling my guts about Mikey, about Josh, about feeling abandoned by the team, even about Lodestone coming up to me. The entire time, Todd peppered the back of my neck with ghostly little kisses, sometimes just resting his lips against the soft skin back there, holding me close the entire time.

I'd never been held like that by someone who cared. It was...amazing. He didn't try to fix things, he just listened. Somehow that helped shrink the things that had infuriated me earlier, the things that made me run from my coach and teammates, back down to size. Maybe they were not so bad, after all. Was this what having a boyfriend would be like? Was this what I'd been missing?

Todd groaned, burying his face against my back. "Aww, Remy. You're killing me."

I scooted back against him, suddenly desperate for closer contact. "What? How?"

"You make me want things with you I can't have."

I thought I knew what he meant. I craned my head back to kiss him. "You mean like something besides a hurried encounter in an unused campsite?"

Todd's shoulders slumped. "Yeah, that."

He sounded a little sad, but I still felt something poking me. "I know what you mean, but it doesn't mean I'd turn down that encounter."

"Does this mean someone's feeling better about things?"

"I'm feeling really good about at least one thing." I reached behind me to feel him. "Whoa. You really live up to that picture."

"Yeah? Think you can take it?"

I turned around so I could kiss him properly. "I know I'm going to try. I hope you thought to bring something to get me ready, because I can't take that monster dry."

"Then it's a good thing I was a Boy Scout, isn't it?" Todd said before he captured my mouth. Funny, but his kisses weren't scary at all. He ran his hands down my chest before he pulled the top of my uni down. I wondered how much I'd be left wearing before he was done with me.

I broke the kiss. "You clean?"

"Yeah, you?" he said breathlessly.

"As a whistle."

*

I jogged back to Cap City's staging area in a melancholy mood. I knew exactly what Todd had meant by wanting things he couldn't have. He made me want to keep something going long-distance for the next year and then apply to Iowa State, just so we could be together. I hadn't said anything about that to him. I needed to think about it first, maybe talk to Goff about it, but damn. We seemed to click on a bunch of levels—

"Where've you been?" Mikey hissed. "You launch now!"

"Wait, what?" I stopped. He grabbed my arm, but I yanked it out of his grip. So much for feeling better about things. What was it about Mikey that made me angry all over again? That boy got under my skin like nothing else.

"There's no time to explain. Cisco still isn't here. You're in his boat, which you would know if you hadn't been AWOL, debasing yourself up against a tree," Mikey hissed.

"What I do or don't do, Michael Castelreigh, is none of your goddamn business, whether it involves trees or not," I snapped, "because as you may or may not recall, you rejected me. As for AWOL, I rowed my race. The last I'd heard, when I put my boat in slings without any help from anyone on this so-called team, I was entered in only one race, a race which I won. Perhaps someday you'll know what a win at Nationals feels like, but until that far-off day, you can blow yourself straight to hell. And it wasn't a tree, it was a picnic table."

Mikey flinched. "Remy...I'm...I'm sorry. You and I have unfinished business, but now's not the time. Lodestone needs you."

I was still mad at Mikey, still furious at Lodestone even. I'm not sure I'd have peed on Mikey if he were burning, but Lodestone? I knew I'd still walk through fire a hundred times over for him, even if I was angry at him, even if I'd taken off on him. I ran for Cap City's boats.

"Thank God," Lodestone said when I ran up. "I need you to jump in the pair for Cisco."

"What? I can't row a pair."

Lodestone shook his head. "Not now, Remy. Just do it. I have to go beg the race organizers to allow the substitution."

"Coach. I don't row pairs. I can't. You know that."

Suddenly Lodestone looked about a thousand years old. "Remy, you're my best rower. You can row anything, and you know it. Right now, Cisco needs you more than you'll ever know, and so do I."

Which was how I ended up in a pair, a configuration I hated, with Todd sticking to my back. Mikey knew it and gave me a look of purest disgust, but worst of all, Lodestone seemed to know it, and that cut like a thousand knives. It might've been a river launch without a dock, but no amount of water could wash away how disgusted I was with myself, by myself, just then.

I'd already downed a sports drink to recover electrolytes after my race, and that plus the run and stretches were going to have to count as my recovery. Jack and I had just enough time for some power pieces on the way to the starting line.

"Nice job, you sick fuck," Jack hissed once we were on the water. I guess he knew what I'd been up to, as well.

"Shut it." The one thing he'd overlooked when he mouthed off was that Cisco had been the stroke and now I was. I might've already raced today, and while Jack was fresh, I was furious. My revenge would take the form of a punishing stroke rating.

Then we were at the starting line and ready to go. "We're rowing this between a thirty-six and a thirty-eight, asshole," I said to Jack. "Try not to fuck it up."

"What! I can't—"

I smiled, but it lacked all humor or mirth. "You *will*. First thirty strokes at a thirty-eight, settle to a thirty-six, bitch."

"No way." He smacked the back of my head, but I didn't care.

"There's no pace but suicide pace, Jack."

"We have alignment," the starter said through her bullhorn.

Jack spat in the water. "Fuck you."

"This is for Cisco. I'll kill you if I have to."

"Ready all! Row!"—*Git, y'all!*—came the starter's call, and we were off.

My legs burned right after that start, but I would've died before I called the stroke rating down. I had something to prove, and Jack needed to back up his attitude with performance or quit rowing. Besides, my coach had said he needed me, and I'd have done almost anything for Cisco.

By seven hundred and fifty meters, I knew only pain—pain in my legs, pain in my lungs, pain in my hands as I tore them to shreds on the oar handle. I didn't care.

By a thousand meters, I heard Jack gasp, "Remy... *please.*"

I grinned. I lived for this.

"Cisco," I gasped.

By fifteen hundred meters, Jack was sobbing.

I became a death eater then, punishing Jack, punishing myself.

"Thirty-eight... Lengthen in two... One...two... Now!"

Now I am become Death.

My vision tunneled down. I saw only the water in our lane.

"Remy!" Jack cried.

The destroyer of rowers.

"There's…line! Empty…it!"

I saw only the red haze of blood. Then I heard the air horn signaling we had crossed the line. Jack and I dropped our oars. I fell backward, gasping for breath, gasping for life. Our boat drifted.

"Cap City, check it down."

I couldn't have cared less. Jack vomited over the gunwales.

"Cap City, check it down now. Acknowledge."

I sat up, my lips and hands numb, my vision blurry.

"Cap City, you are heading for the dam's spillway. Check it down or forfeit."

I roused myself from my stupor enough to raise my hand. "Check it down," I mumbled to Jack.

"Huh?" he said, just as groggy as I.

"Check it down," I said sharply. "The refs are pissed."

Over the PA I heard the ref chuckle. "That, ladies and gentlemen, is giving it your all. Are you boys all right?"

I waved listlessly and then gave the commands to turn our boat and take it back to Cap City's place on the beach. As we rowed past, bystanders in the grandstands and along the beach clapped, but I was too wiped to care. The announcer said something else, something about us and our row, but it was nothing more than a buzz in the background.

"You, Remy, are an asshole," Jack said, "but a damn good rower. Dude... I think we won."

"Whatever." I was too dead to care.

"Remy...is something wrong?" Jack said.

I turned to look at him. "Like you even care."

"Asshole."

"If it's not rowing, it's not my concern," I said as we climbed into the water.

He sighed behind me. "You really do operate on a different plane from the rest of us, don't you?"

This time our team actually met us. I regarded them like a sovereign does his subjects because I had nothing left to give anyone. "Deal with it."

"Dude..." Mikey breathed as I brushed by.

"Don't even." There was only one person I would talk to right then. "Where is he?"

"Who?" Mikey said.

I looked at him like he was stupid. At least he was smart enough to figure it out. "Oh. At the judges' tent."

I grabbed another sports drink and some flip-flops. I hoped they were mine. I was in no mood to deal with anyone I didn't have to, and right then I was stalking my coach.

I caught up to Lodestone, and yes, he was right where Mikey had indicated.

One of the USRowing referees spotted me before Lodestone did. "Congratulations, young man. That was quite a performance," she said, shaking my hand.

"Thank you, ma'am."

The referee, an older woman, looked grave. "A tragic situation, very unfortunate."

I'd only ever heard the phrase "blood ran cold." Just then I lived it. "Then you know more than I do, ma'am. This was the hottest hot seating I've ever done. All my coach told me was that he and Cisco needed me more than they ever have before."

"I'd better let your coach fill you in, Mr. Babcock. Under the circumstances, we allowed the substitution, but your performance made them both proud. We awarded three medals in this case."

"Thank you again, Maryanne," Lodestone said. "I've got some news to deliver."

The referee nodded. "I understand."

"Coach? What's going on?" My fury drained away, leaving only fear.

He wiped a tear away. "Let's find somewhere private, okay?"

As we walked, he put an arm around my shoulder. "Sometimes I really hate being an adult."

We ended up sitting in the shade of a tree far away from the tumult of the regatta. "Please, Coach, can you tell me what's happening? You and that ref, you're kind of scaring me."

"I'm sorry, Remy. That was never the intention." Lodestone sighed. "First of all, your race was amazing. I get that you were pretty angry—"

"I was furious. Jack mouthed off once we were out of range—"

Lodestone snorted. "You weren't out of range, and I'll deal with him. Let's just say sound carries on the water."

"Yeah? Well, we raced at a thirty-eight for most of that piece."

"I know. I counted. You looked good. He looked miserable." Lodestone grinned and held up a stopwatch. "Anyway, it was a good race, and if you haven't figured it out, you won. Two golds today, Remy. I told you, you can row anything. Next year, you're rowing small boats for any race that has them, but that's not the point. I owe you an explanation."

"Cisco," I whispered.

He nodded. "Cisco. After your race in the single, I got a call from a member of Cisco's family, one of his older brothers. His parents were running late, speeding to get here. They were in an accident."

I gasped. "No."

"His parents didn't make it. Died at the scene. Cisco was airlifted to the Med Center and was in surgery." Lodestone choked up. I could tell he was fighting not to cry. "His...his brother knew how important this was to him and called me. His little brother was on the table and fighting for his life, and he called me to tell me that Cisco was in surgery."

We both lost it at that point. After Lodestone recovered enough to talk, he said, "He didn't make it, Remy. He's gone."

We didn't return to the boats for a long time. Mikey stomped up to me when Lodestone and I trudged back, but one look at our red eyes and he backed off, a question on his face. All I could do was shake my head and clutch my gold medals, which meant nothing that afternoon. Maybe later they would. I sat numbly on a bench. I thought I heard someone yell something about getting off my ass, but Lodestone bit his head off. Then the poor man took Jack aside and got to repeat the bad news all over again.

The referees made an announcement about Cisco, however, and the regatta observed a moment of silence. A rower had died on the way to the races, and that lightning-fast pair? That had been a race in his honor. It hadn't been in Cisco's honor at the time, but it helped Cap City's legend and made a fitting memorial for my friend. Rowing had no tradition to honor our dead, so it wasn't like people saluted or anything, but Cap City—juniors and masters—would honor Cisco later.

Mikey pried my phone away from me and called Goff. Goff and my dad drove up to get me. Todd came and held me as long as he could, but ultimately, he had responsibilities of his own. Then Mikey took over. I remember Goff driving me home in our car while Dad drove home in his. I felt safe letting go in front of him and telling him about the accident, because he knew Cisco too. Mom was waiting for us when we pulled up, and I was never so glad to be around my family as I was that afternoon. My family circled the wagons around me and allowed me to let go in a way I hadn't since I was little. I remembered the phones ringing too much, my cell phone as well as the home line, but Mom unplugged the landlines and Goff took control of my cell phone. Goff also undressed me and made me shower. He dried me off and made me go to bed too. Mom cancelled everything, and surprisingly, she stayed home from work for a few days to take care of me. I'd never lost a friend like that before, and I didn't know what to do. Dad did, however. He was a shrink, after all.

Chapter Twelve

After giving me a few days to recover physically and emotionally, days in which Cisco's funeral had been scheduled and Dad had dragged me and Goff out to buy new suits since ours no longer fit, Goff moved in for the kill. I was sure he didn't see it that way, but that was how it felt.

We lazed around the pool in the backyard. It wasn't much of a pool, but then, the yard wasn't that big either. Land cost too much for huge lots in California, or at least in Davis. Smallish yards meant small pools. We could get wet, but it wasn't good for swimming laps or anything.

"So," Goff said, paddling his inflatable raft over to where I rested in the shade, "who was that guy holding you before Mikey took over?"

Aww, jeez, so much for dodging that bullet. "What guy?"

"Don't play dumb." Goff splashed me. It actually felt pretty good.

I started thinking about Todd. We had continued to text and had even added Skype after the regatta. I missed him. A lot.

"Oh. My. God."

I looked up at Goff. He sported the biggest shit-eating grin I had ever seen in my life. "What?"

"My brother's got a crush on a guy. The great ice prince falls."

I made a face. "Your obscene gloating is very unbecoming."

"Oh no, you don't," Goff said. He cackled with glee. "You're not going to wriggle out of this that easily."

"I could roll off this and swim for a while. You'd never believe how long I can hold my breath," I said hopefully.

Goff rolled his eyes. "You'd have to surface sooner or later, and if you're down there too long, I'll get the skimmer and fish you out. Now talk."

"His name's Todd Nelson, and he's an assistant coach for another team. Before you get too excited, he's only eighteen, so it's not creepy or anything." I let myself smile at the thought of him. "He's the closest I've had to a boyfriend, I guess."

"That's great, Remy. I'm happy for you. So, where'd you meet him?"

It was a logical question, but somehow, I felt defensive. "Um...online?"

"Is that a question or a statement?" Goff said.

Maybe I could pretend my embarrassment was an impending sunburn. "A statement," I said with a sigh. "We met online, Grindr, actually. We're just friends, really, but by the time the Nationals rolled around, we both realized it could be so much more."

"That's great, Remy. So, what's the problem?"

"He lives in Iowa."

"Oh."

"Yeah, 'oh' is right. It totally sucks too. I meet someone I really like, and he lives half a continent away." I threw an arm over my eyes, like I could block out the truth along with the sunlight or something.

"Very nice," Goff said. He sounded far too content for what was basically a sucky situation for me, and I said as much. "Okay, no, the fact that this Todd person lives so far away isn't good, but the fact that you found someone who—ahem—floats your boat, that's good, right? I've been worried about you, Germy. You've always been so aloof, and that's not what I want for you. A crush is better than nothing."

I sat up. "It is not a crush. Is Laurel a crush?"

"No, she's not."

I chucked an empty soda can at him. I missed by miles. I should've put water in it. "Damn straight."

"As it were." Goff snorted. "But long-distance. That's rough."

"I know. Do...do you think I'm crazy for considering applying to the school he goes to?"

Goff tilted his head like he always did when he thought about something. "Not necessarily. How long did you two get to know each other before the race? Two weeks?"

I shook my head. "Most of the summer, but it was all online."

"By itself, that's not enough, but if you can keep the flame going all next year? I don't see why you shouldn't head out there," Goff said. "I mean, one school's pretty much the same as another for undergrad education, isn't it?"

"I guess so." The fact that Goff didn't think I was totally insane made me happy.

"Wait, Germy, did you say Grindr?" I knew it had been too good to last.

"Yeah, but that shouldn't matter, should it?" I really didn't want to talk about that anymore.

Goff shook his head. "Jeez, that's basically a germ farm, right? A Petri dish?"

"How do you know all this?" I asked with a sinking feeling. Because he was right.

"My brother's gay. I'm educating myself."

I thought about it. For some reason, I felt the need to tell him everything. Maybe after the regatta and Lodestone's look when I came back from meeting Todd, it was time to come clean.

"Let's go inside. This isn't something that needs to be broadcast to the neighborhood."

"All right," Goff said, looking at me closely, like he could see the dirt on me, which was absurd. I wasn't dirty. I wasn't morally unclean. I wasn't even germ-ridden. So why did I feel like I had to confess?

After we had dried ourselves off, we flopped out in my room. "So...my summer activities."

"I assume this is beyond work, school, and rowing?" Goff said, raising an eyebrow.

I nodded. "You assume correctly. I've been a busy boy."

And with that, I told my brother how I'd learned my way around men's bodies. I spared him some details, but I made my point.

To Goff's credit and my surprise, all he said was, "Were you safe? What about condoms? Our stash didn't go down that fast. Were you using them?"

"I made sure the guys were clean."

Goff narrowed his eyes. "How?"

"I asked them." Funny how I'd felt that was enough all summer, but I was suddenly afraid of talking to my brother. "Besides, even if they had it, if they were on meds, they couldn't pass it on."

Goff shook his head. "Dude, I don't think that's how it works," he whispered. "I'm going to check with Laurel. And Remy? I think you should get tested."

I didn't need to ask him for what.

*

"How're you holding up?" Todd said. We were on Skype again. He wanted a lot more of my time after Nationals, or so it seemed.

I smiled—or tried to. "I'm okay. Cisco's funeral's tomorrow. That's going to be rough."

"I wish I could be there to support you." He looked worried.

"I'll be okay." What choice did I have? "I'm more worried about what's left of his family, you know? Both parents, plus Cisco? He has—had—a younger sister. What's going to happen to her?"

Todd frowned. "That's rough. Any relatives close by?"

"A couple of older siblings, including the one who called my coach while I was racing my single. It's not like she'll be at the mercy of the system or anything, but still. That's a lot of loss for one family."

"It is indeed."

We deliberately moved the conversation into safer waters after that, or at least less emotionally fraught waters. You can only talk about death for so long, even the death of a friend. But I soon realized rowing and that one hookup were really all we had in common, and even I got tired of talking about rowing.

Then Todd grew still. "Who's that?"

"What? Who's who?" I looked around. The only person in the room was Goff, and all he was doing was reading on my bed.

"That guy in your room." Todd looked pissed, like crazy jealous pissed.

I felt rather than saw Goff sit up behind me. I think he snickered.

"That's my brother," I said, laughing.

Todd's eyes narrowed, like he didn't believe me. "You never said you had a brother."

"No, but I never said I didn't either. Jeez, calm down. Geoff, meet Todd. Todd, this is Geoff, my twin brother."

"You two look nothing alike." Todd was turning redder by the minute, and I was suddenly glad he lived halfway across the country.

"Did I say identical twin? No, I did not. You really need to calm down. Even if I weren't—"

"Pardon me, Germy," Goff said. He held his iPhone up to the camera on my computer. "Excuse the small print but check it out. It's the wiki entry for 'fraternal twins.' Read it. Absorb it. Become one with it. Then have a little more respect for my brother, asshole."

"Germy?" Todd's eyes had gone flat.

"My full name is Jeremy, and believe it or not, brothers sometimes have nicknames for each other." I realized I was speaking very slowly, as if Todd's comprehension was in question. It might sound patronizing, but right then I didn't care. "It really doesn't matter if you believe Geoff and I are fraternal twins or not. Even if he were just a friend, I get to have those too. It's not like we're boyfriends, so I'm not sure where you're getting this jealousy bullshit? But it needs to go back there."

"I have to go," Todd said.

I nodded. "I think that's a good idea."

"I've got a boyfriend," he blurted suddenly.

Goff appeared back over my shoulder. "What?"

"Get him out of here," Todd snapped.

"No, he's fine where he is," I said. "So, about this boyfriend..."

Todd laughed. "Dude, I thought you—"

"Don't 'dude' me. I've got all our texts. You never said a damn thing about a boyfriend." I had a feeling this was more about Todd's jealousy and less about a boyfriend, real or imagined.

"It's not like it matters."

I thought about it for a short while. "It would've to me. We wouldn't have hooked up, for starters."

Todd didn't say anything, but I suddenly didn't like the whole vibe of our interaction since the Youth Nationals. I reached for the keyboard to disconnect the conversation. "Lose my number."

Todd looked panic-stricken. "Remy, wait! I'm sorry, I didn't mean—"

I cut him off and deleted the app from my desktop.

Goff, still standing behind me, said, "I know that must've hurt, but I think you did the right thing."

"I don't really know what just happened, but I'm younger than Todd, so why am I older than he is?"

"Remy," Goff said, putting his hand on my shoulder, "you've never been young, not once in your whole life."

*

The day after Cisco's funeral, Cap City honored his passing with a ceremony on the dock. Lodestone had already hung his portrait and a framed copy of his obituary along with his honorary medal in the pairs at the back of the boathouse. That made me sad. Within a few years, no one would know who he had been, the chemicals in his picture would turn and the portrait fade, the obituary's cheap newsprint would yellow, and then it would all end up in a drawer.

With those depressing thoughts on my mind, I sat on the dock watching the setting sun and waiting for Lodestone, who'd said he wanted to speak to me. I was probably ruining my suit, but whatever. Maybe if I looked hard enough into the setting sun...

Lodestone sat down beside me, rubbing his hand over his face, like he was tired or something. Then again, the Nationals were over, and it occurred to me he'd put at least as much energy into this as we rowers had. Everyone was tired.

"Remy..." He paused, and I realized he was red under his tan and not from the August heat. "I nominated myself for this because I'm your coach, but I'm also hoping in a way I'm still your friend and because I doubt very much you've spoken to your parents about this."

I cringed. I knew where this was going. "Coach, please...don't."

"Remy... Jeremy, I think I have to. After a certain conversation with Josh Brennan, as well as my own observations, I have an idea what some of your leisure-time activities might've been—might be—this summer."

"This isn't any of your business." I stood up—or tried. Lodestone put his hand on my arm. Damn, he was strong.

"Sit down, Remy. Please. This isn't an inquisition or anything, and I'm not going to run to your parents. I'm worried about you." Lodestone sighed. "Your sexual orientation isn't a secret around the boathouse and wasn't before the Crew Classic in April. I know you're gay, and hopefully you know by now that I don't care, but you're doing some risky things, and I need—as your friend—to make sure you're taking care of yourself."

I swallowed the lump in my throat. "What do you mean, risky?"

"That you can say that tells me I'm way too late." He closed his eyes for a moment. "Sabrina would be far better suited for this. She's a nurse, you know. I'm glad I asked her—"

I jumped to my feet. "That's it. I'm out of here—"

"Sit!" That time he didn't place his hand on my arm, he clamped on to me and forced me back down. "I didn't name names, I just told her I needed information. You should know by now that you're not the only gay rower. Neither you nor Mikey, for that matter. Remy, there's nothing intrinsically wrong with what you're doing, but you've got to take care of yourself. Has anyone ever talked to you about safer sex?" Lodestone said.

"I've heard the term, but that's like, from the '80s or something, right?" Suddenly this whole conversation made me very uncomfortable.

"That's when it started, yes," Lodestone said, "but it's still very real. How about negotiated risk?"

I shook my head. Something told me I might've made a lot of mistakes this summer.

"Okay, Remy, what do the words 'safer sex' mean to you?"

I thought about it for a few moments. "Condoms, mostly. But that's for older guys, like older than you. AIDS is practically curable now, and if you don't play with older guys, there's almost no chance of getting it."

"Oh, Remy." Lodestone looked sad, like someone just kicked his dog. "Nothing could be further from the truth. So, what does negotiated risk mean?"

"I know what the words mean, but apparently not what they mean in terms of this conversation." Honestly, what was he getting at?

"It means you and your partner decide together before—got that, *before*—you're intimate what level of risk of exposure to HIV you'll accept." Lodestone looked me in the eyes, and his were bright, like maybe he was trying not to cry. "Some acts are inherently riskier than others, and strangers generally accept less risk than committed partners. This isn't just a gay thing, Remy. My girlfriend and I went through all of this, too, and—get this through your head—HIV isn't the only sexually transmitted disease out there."

I didn't know what to say. I wanted to deny all of it. "I'm all right. Everyone said they were clean, Coach."

"You'd better hope they were telling you the truth. You'd better hope they knew the truth themselves, because according to the CDC, most people don't." Lodestone stood up. "Think about what I've said, okay, Remy?"

Like I would've been able to do anything else. "Thanks, Coach. I... Yeah. I'll be thinking about it."

Chapter Thirteen

Todd tried to text me a few more times, but I ignored him. Then Goff showed me how to block his number. I suppose I could have tried to reason with him, but after talking it over with my brother, I decided I didn't need to deal with that kind of bone-deep crazy. Anyone who freaked out because my *brother* was in my room when I spoke to him was not someone I needed in my life. I felt nothing but relief that I had never brought up applying to Todd's school or trying to keep something going long-distance to anyone but Goff.

The last few weeks before my senior year looked to be slow ones, just sculling to stay in shape and light weights at the gym, nothing exciting. Crew resumed regular practices that consisted only of easy, steady-state rowing to ease those who hadn't rowed at Nationals back into the groove. That was most of the team, and true to his word, Lodestone kept me in the single. I enjoyed rowing circles—literal circles—around the big boats. I think Lodestone enjoyed watching it too.

I caught up on pleasure reading, a relief to read for fun instead of necessity. Goff had also cut back on his activities, although football started to ramp up and much more intensely than crew. So, while seeing Goff and spending time at home with him was great, he was dog-tired most of the time.

Seeing Mikey at practice raised specters I thought had been laid to rest. Naïve of me, I suppose. He always looked like he had something he wanted to say to me too. Since I rowed in a single, I usually managed to be off the water and out of there before he could corner me. The last time he'd cornered me, he'd given me an earful about my mating habits right before what had literally been the biggest race of the year. Since his timing and choice of subject sucked, I didn't see the point of a repeat performance.

Then he cornered me. "You're a slippery one."

"Well, you know, Astroglide." Damnation. I knew I'd gone too far down the river during practice, but the water had been perfect. As a result, I found Mikey sitting on the hood of my car after practice. Sure, it had been a cheap comment, but his consternation made it worthwhile.

Mikey shook his head. "Why do you always make things so difficult?"

"Me? That shoe fits you, Cinderella," I said, jerking the car door open. "Now please, get off my car."

"Actually, you have to give me a ride home. My ride already left." He didn't even look apologetic. In fact, he looked pretty damn smug.

"I should make you walk."

"But you won't, will you?"

I smirked at him and drove off. The sight of him standing there, mouth agape, in my rearview mirror was one I'd treasure forever.

Oh, I knew I would give him a ride home, but there was no way I'd reward that kind of behavior without making him sweat for it. Actually, all I did was drive until I was out of view and then text him.

REMY: Get up here, you fucker.

Then I opened the passenger door so there could be no mistaking my intent.

"You're an asshole, you know that?"

"But I notice you're not turning down the ride."

Mikey slammed the door and fastened his seat belt. "I was going to ask if we could talk, but maybe not."

"Is there anything to talk about, Mikey? Really? You've made your feelings about me pretty clear since San Diego," I said. "I have to be honest. It's sucked."

"That's what I want to talk about," he whispered.

We drove back to Davis in silence. I didn't look at him, no side-eye action or anything, but my mind raced about a million miles an hour.

"Can we go to your house?" Mikey said.

"Why?"

He sighed. "Because I need to talk to you and my dad's working from home today."

"Very well. My parents are at work and Goff's at football practice."

"I know." Mikey gloated. "I already cleared it with him."

I shook my head. "Do I even want to know?"

"Probably not."

I parked the car in front of the house. My parents didn't ask for a whole lot from me and Goff, but they were pretty insistent that the driveway and garage belonged to their cars. It was hard to argue with that.

I sat on the hood of my car. "So...here we are. Start talking."

"You're not going to invite me in?" Mikey didn't sound all that serious, like he knew he had already pushed me further than was wise.

"Fine. We can go sit in the backyard," I said, dragging him around back through the side gate. I motioned to one of the loungers on the deck as I took one myself. "Start talking."

Mikey sat down and took a few minutes to gather his thoughts. "First, I'm sorry for the way I've been acting all summer."

I blinked. "Okay, that's not what I expected to hear."

"I know." He smiled sadly. "I've been doing a lot of thinking, and I'm sorry for overreacting. Do you have any idea how much it hurt to see you whoring yourself out to that guy—what was his name, Josh?—all summer? I wish it had been me, but it seemed like you hated me."

I saw red, and before I knew what I was doing, I had surged up and out of the lounger. I loomed over him, my hands on either armrest.

"Hey, I get that you're angry, but step off," he said.

I backed up, but I was still livid. "I am not," I hissed through clenched teeth, "a whore. If you ever call me that again, I will kick your nose in. And in case you've forgotten a few key facts, *Mikey*, let me remind you that I all but threw myself at you earlier this summer. You had your goddamn chance. 'Right guy at the right time,' remember? You turned me down, and it burned like the heart of the sun. I've spent the summer running from that."

Mikey jumped to his feet. "I was scared, okay? Is that all right with the emotionally invulnerable über-rower who scares the crap out of the rest of us on the water? The guy I've wanted since I met him? Then you threw yourself at me, and it scared the hell out of me. Then I had to watch you all summer being with everyone but me, and how do you think that made me feel?" As he yelled at me, he moved closer and closer, backing me into the wall of my house until we were nose to nose, chest to chest. "I never got another chance, and my name is Michael," he all but screamed. "If you don't stop calling me Mikey, I will end you."

Mikey liked me? "I...I never knew."

He laughed bitterly. "Of course, you didn't. You never gave me a chance to explain, and I was as much of a mess emotionally as you were, especially knowing I'm the one who encouraged you to call Josh."

His hands were on either side of my head, and his chest pressed mine back into the wall, and it was impossible to process what he said. "Um, Mikey—Michael—I can't really think when you're doing that," I said, my voice rough.

"Oh. Oh! You like this, do you?" Michael growled in my ear. "You like it like this?"

"Uh...yes?" I squeaked. I had barely figured it out over the summer, but somehow, suddenly, Michael was hitting every button I had, and I thought my mind would never function again.

He smirked. "Rough, but not roughed up?"

I nodded slowly.

"I can work with that. Now open the door."

Then Michael frog-marched me upstairs to my bedroom. When the hell had he hit puberty because damn, was he strong. On the way, he grabbed a few rubbers from the stash, just in case. "How'd you know about those?"

"Geoff."

I shook my head, trying to clear it of the Michael-induced buzz. I guess I had always suspected he had a crush on me but figured he had managed to cure himself after the Crew Classic. But there was nothing like a guy pinning you to a wall and growling in your ear to confirm he still had a thing for you. And yeah, he had grown at least an inch, and his shoulders had gotten broader. No wonder he had been cranky lately. Growing would do that.

You could never eat or sleep enough, your joints always hurt, and your coordination was shot to hell.

The best part of all was that Michael liked to cuddle. So that time Goff had walked in on us, he hadn't been wrong, just premature. While he held me, I leveled with him about my summer, not the gory details, just the highlights.

I shrugged, suddenly shy about it. "I think I was about at the end of it. Todd had helped me figure that much out."

"How so?" Michael looked down at me while stroking my hair.

I looked up at him. "It feels good physically, but it's lonely. Tricks don't hold you afterward."

Michael kissed the top of my head. "I'm sorry."

"Don't be." I reached up and pulled him down so I could kiss him.

I didn't know about older or wiser, but I felt like I'd learned a lesson or two over the past couple of months, and I spent the rest of the summer happily exploring this new version of Michael Castelreigh. He seemed just as enamored of me. Let Goff exhaust himself with football practice. Michael and I spent our fast-dwindling summer on leisurely rows and each other.

*

We rechristened the car the "Love Boat" on the first day of school because its occupants were two couples and two of us were rowers. That it was white didn't hurt either. Goff helpfully pointed out that I was a princess.

I was shy about it at first, but Michael dragged my arm around his shoulder, and as I was quickly learning, Michael was very assertive and toppy. As I was also learning, I liked it that way. We earned a few raised eyebrows, but Michael acted like he was impervious, and I learned to ignore them. Eventually. A few people made rude comments, and even though I wanted to hide, I didn't. We got a few wolf whistles, generally from other Cap City rowers who'd watched us last spring, along with "About time, you two!" Those felt good.

"I told you it'd be fine," Michael said, giving me a quick peck on my cheek.

I blushed. I didn't know I still could.

Michael chuckled. "You're so adorkable."

The first week of school was borderline useless as far as academics went, and clubs and other application fluffers didn't really crank up until the third week.

"Do I have to be out at school?" I complained.

Michael gave me a very convincing facsimile of the evil eye. "Yes." I still must've looked rebellious because he leaned over and whispered in my ear. "I'll reward you as soon as we get back to your place after practice."

I swallowed. I didn't know where Michael got his ideas. Either he had a lurid imagination, or he watched a lot of porn. I wasn't sure which one intrigued me more.

So that was how Michael dragged me into the GSA meeting. Much to my surprise, Goff and Laurel were already there. I would've said something about irony, but Goff had already made it clear to me that he was educating himself about all things gay because of me, and Laurel was obviously an advocate too. I wondered if she had someone in her family who was LGBT. I also wondered why I had never asked her. Was I really that absorbed by rowing? I would've asked Michael, but he'd just tousle my hair or kiss me or something and then laugh.

Similarly, while on-the-water practices at Cap City increased in intensity after school started, the real testing for who would row where started only during the third week.

"Okay, as you know, it's erg testing today," Lodestone called, trying with only limited success to overcome the noise of chatting teenagers in a boathouse with a concrete floor. "This is preliminary, and nothing today is set in stone, so even if you crater, you'll have plenty of time to bring your time down. But we need a place to start, and today's it."

I hated erg testing, and based on the look Michael shot me, he felt the same way. In fact, no one on either the boys' varsity or junior varsity liked erg tests. This one was a 6k test, six thousand meters in purgatory but not true hell. The strategy behind an early-season test was to give it your almost-all, to be tapped out but not riding the vomit comet, if only because reality entailed beating the resulting score in a few weeks, or so it seemed to me. Part of my game for each season was to show steady improvement with each test. I refused to accept a plateau, and a slower score on a test sparked endless self-loathing. I hadn't done that since my novice year.

Someone put Outbreak Monkey on the sound system, and then we all sat on our ergs at the catch positions, just like in the boats.

"Ready all!" Lodestone called. "Row!"

I set out at a few seconds per five hundred meters slower than my usual 6k pace, my standard practice for this sort of test early in the season.

By two thousand meters into the test, I knew I was in trouble. I felt like I hadn't rowed all summer, like I had done nothing to stay in shape since San Diego. What the hell?

I tried to maintain my pace, but within another five hundred meters, I knew I had to back off or stop rowing, and not even my fury at the thought of slowing provided enough fuel for me to keep going. Worse, I kept having to slow down. By the time I slumped over at the end, I had pulled a time almost as slow as that one my novice year.

Lodestone leaned over to look at the monitor. "Remy? Are you all right?"

"No, not really." I sighed and then looked up at my coach. "I can't rest up. No matter what I do, I'm always tired."

Lodestone nodded. "Talk to me after practice."

I grabbed some water and texted Goff to let him know I'd be a few minutes late.

"What happened?" Michael said as people filtered out of the boathouse.

I shrugged. "I was too tired to pull anything resembling a reasonable erg score."

"That's not like you. Lodestone wants to talk to you?"

"Of course."

"I'll wait out of the way."

"That's okay," I said. "There's no reason you can't hear this, I don't think."

Finally, Lodestone was ready for me. "So, talk to me, Remy. What happened?"

"Beats me." I sighed. "I'm tired all the time. It was a hellacious summer in terms of physical activity—"

Michael snorted, but Lodestone rolled his eyes.

"You know, it's entirely possible you're depressed," Lodestone said. "A good friend and teammate died during the Nationals, and you had to jump in to take his place without warning. Sure, you pulled off a virtuoso performance, but that doesn't change the fact that he died."

I opened my mouth and then closed it. I'd never considered the possibility. Cisco and I were friends, good friends even, but I'd never thought of us as besties. It was something to talk over with Michael and Goff, maybe even my dad. He was a psychotherapist, after all.

"That had never occurred to me."

"Give it some thought," Lodestone said. "Or you might just be exhausted. You set a punishing schedule for yourself this summer, and the month or so between Nationals and school weren't really much of a break, not with the demands you placed on your body." He thought for a moment. "Oh! Something else to consider. You could have your iron checked. Athletes have different iron demands than nonathletes, so what counts as anemic for us is different. Be sure to include your ferritin levels. No one ever tests for it, but it's important. In fact, right after the blood test, go ahead and start supplementing your iron. Don't wait for the labs. You're active and growing. It won't hurt."

I nodded. "Got it. Rest up, be depressed, have my iron checked, take pills for it."

"I'm not sure that's how I put it," Lodestone said, looking pained, "but yes."

Michael put his arm around me as we headed out to the car. He liked to do that, I'd noticed, and I realized I liked him to, but just before I left the boathouse, I looked over my shoulder and caught Lodestone's eye. He looked thoughtful, thoughtful and worried. I didn't need to ask why.

Chapter Fourteen

Some things never changed in the Babcock household, like my mother and her nearly single-minded determination that her sons make the world a better place for those who might never otherwise go to the prom. What Goff and I could never figure out was why she fixated on the *junior* prom. We didn't mind, we just couldn't figure it out.

Goff, Laurel, Michael, and I had taken over the living room one evening in early September to study. The Davis High grind was well under way, and we figured if we ever wanted to see each other, parallel play while studying was the only way.

Mom brought us dinner, which should have been my first clue that she was building up to something. Goff shot me several significant looks, but as usual I missed them, since they had nothing to do with rowing.

Michael nudged me. "I think Goff's trying to get your attention."

"What?" I blinked, looking up from my O-chem text.

Goff nodded. "Don't you think it's odd she's catering our study session? School's starting, and you know what that means, don't you?"

"Um...homework? Tests?" I said, floundering.

Proms, you fool, Goff texted.

Suffering Christ, I fired back.

I looked up to see Laurel and Michael snickering at each other.

As if Goff had summoned her, Mom came back into the living room. "Geoffrey, Jeremy, I'd like to talk to you about something important."

"Yeah, Mom?" I said, looking up, joined shortly by Goff.

"I know it's just September, but it's never too soon to start thinking about the junior prom," our mother said. "Now I'm sorry, Laurel. I know you and Geoff are going steady..."

Mom burbled on, but I mouthed "going steady" to Goff as Michael elbowed me in a pointless attempt to force me to behave. He should've known better by then.

"...but I think you'll agree that something like this, that strikes a blow for all womankind, is so much more important. Besides, Jeremy, you're not currently seeing anyone that I know of, so it shouldn't be too great a hardship for you."

By this time, Goff and Laurel were biting their lips to keep from exploding into hysterical laughter, because they knew full well who I was seeing and that he was rolling his eyes at my mother's spiel. The outrageousness of it all was enough to keep them from puking at Mom's nonsense about splitting them up in the name of social engineering.

Meanwhile, Michael, who was sitting close enough not even the holy spirit could've fit between us, texted me.

MICHAEL: *Strike a blow, Remy.*

As the apparently unattached member of the Babcock family present for this farce, it fell to me to disabuse Mom of her delusions. I finally pushed Michael, who was shaking so hard it annoyed me, away.

"The problem with that, Mom, is that it's the *junior* prom, as in organized by and for the junior class. As seniors, if Geoff and I go, it'll be because we're invited by juniors. Since he's dating a fellow senior, I'm thinking that's not going to happen," I said.

Mom pouted, a surprisingly unattractive look. "You could..."

Michael growled, softly but still a growl.

I smiled. "I have a reasonable expectation of being asked, I think."

That was enough for my brother and his girlfriend. They broke and ran for the stairs, howling the entire way.

"I wonder what got into them?" Mom said. "Keep your door open!" she called after them.

"Probably the fact that you keep harping on this. Honestly, Mom, it's not healthy." Mom crossed her arms in a way I knew meant trouble brewing. "Please, Mom. You need to let this go. Geoff and Laurel are *dating*, and you just tried to make it sound rational for him to take someone else to a formal dance."

"But—"

I shook my head. "Mom, you've told me what your high school years were like, and while I sympathize, my brother and I can't rewrite the past."

"It's just a dance." Mom sounded petulant.

Aaand my sympathy ran out as she insisted on being a clownish caricature about this. She was the most rational woman I knew about almost everything else, but this? Whatever, crazy lady. Oh well, they say even the most intelligent, rational of people believe at least one insane thing...

Michael and I managed—somehow—to keep absolutely straight faces. "We might as well go up to my room," I said. "Laurel's in my O-chem class, and if I'm going to study with her, it'll be easier if I'm at least somewhere near her."

So, we gathered up our things while Mom took the dishes to the sink, shaking her head the entire way. Michael and I made it to my bedroom and shut the door before we fell to my bed choking with laughter.

"Bad rower! Bad!" Michael said, kissing my nose and not coincidentally pinning me to my bed. I liked that. A lot.

Goff coughed from the bathroom door, but it's not like he'd interrupted anything, at least not yet.

"Thanks for trying, Remy," Laurel said. She wore a broad grin.

"Shame on you, taking advantage of our mother's weird obsession." Goff wagged his finger at me.

I looked up at him from where Michael had me trapped under him. "Oh, like you wouldn't."

"We're not talking about me," Geoff said like he had some sort of moral ground to stand on. He smiled. "Behave, you two."

"Yeah, right," Michael whispered, diving in for more kisses. I wasted no time in allowing my hands to roam. I liked his geography and took every chance I could to explore it. For all my adventures this summer, I felt strangely reluctant about going certain places, like Michael mattered where those other guys hadn't. When Michael and I were intimate, I wanted it to mean something.

When we were kissed out, at least for the time being, Michael looked down at me with a look in his eyes I hadn't seen before. But I liked it. It made me feel wanted and not just physically.

I smiled up at him. "So...am I officially invited?"

He rolled over next to me and pulled me close. "You are indeed."

"Hmmm, you in a tuxedo," I said. "The thought of that excites me. I don't know if I'll be able to keep my hands off you."

"That works both ways, you know. I get to look at you wrapped up like a present all night, and then you know what I'll get to do?" he said.

"No." I liked where this was going, however.

Michael sat up a little to look at me. "Well, since the prom is less than a month before Christmas, I think I'll unwrap you like the best Christmas present ever."

I swear I choked at the thought. Two hot guys in tuxes teasing each other all night? Okay, one hot guy and me, but still. That image alone would get me through many a lonely night.

"You think..." I started to say but stopped.

"Go on." Michael started to play with my hair, and that usually short-circuited about half of my synapses.

"You think that would be a good time to come out to my parents? That night or sometime around then?"

He nodded slowly. "Seems like as good a time as any." He hesitated. "I know the GSA annoys you, but they'll have some good advice for coming out."

I thought about it for a while. Then something else occurred to me. "Are you out to your parents?"

"Not officially, no, but I've never made a secret of it either." Michael laughed. "I'm not sure what they thought this summer with me alternating between moping around because I'd run you off and then swearing at you because you'd rejected me."

I thought about that for a while. "Depends on how insightful they are. We spent a lot of time together. If they had a clue, they might've figured it out. If they're like mine, they just chalked it up to a busy summer."

"So maybe this would be a good time for us both to come out, then," Michael said softly, looking into my eyes. I smiled back. It was a while before we returned to our homework.

*

My iron panel came back normal, and as near as I could tell, the supplements did nothing. Still, I did my best to eat right and get enough rest, but it was never enough. Fatigue was my constant companion, and even my parents noticed. The only reason they didn't say anything was because Lodestone and I were already taking steps. On my coach's advice, I dropped my weight section. I didn't need the units, it wasn't a requirement to graduate, and it only wore me down further.

There were more pressing issues, like college applications. Lodestone had already been in contact with the crew coaches at the schools that interested me— UCSD, UCLA, UCSB, the University of Washington, and Boston U—so I knew they were interested in me, particularly after my performance at the Nationals. I would've loved to apply to small private schools in New England, but the reality was my parents had two people to put through college at the same time, so the three UCs constituted my practical schools, UW was my crew powerhouse fantasy, and BU was my East Coast dream. I knew CalPac's coach wanted me and had even offered early admission, but I wanted out of the Sacramento area.

All college applications meant were more essays to write on frankly bizarre subjects on top of my schoolwork.

Goff had been forced to pare his list down, too, although he knew he wouldn't be playing football in college. He cheerfully admitted he wasn't that good and wasn't nearly big enough and, in any case, preferred not to risk traumatic brain injury. Sensible one, that Goff. But Goff, like me, had his three practical schools and his pie-in-the-sky schools. If only the University of California gave bulk discounts, because odds were my brother and I would both end up at one or more of the system's campuses.

Of course, my dreams of collegiate crew depended on figuring out why I was so tired. Neither Lodestone nor I could find any good reason, and I finally broke down and asked my parents if I could have a doctor's appointment for a complete physical. My doctor didn't ask about sexual health, even though that seemed kind of obvious to me. I didn't have the nerve to say anything. I knew Goff and Lodestone wanted me to get tested, but I just couldn't. What if I did, and it came back positive? Everything covered on the physical came back normal.

When it came to rowing, since Lodestone had me in small boats, I had some leeway. I rowed in the single to stay in what condition I could, and it was not as if I were exhausted constantly. Some days, even many, were fantastic, but I was fatigued enough to worry me, my parents, and Lodestone. Michael too. It went on long enough that I refused to accept my intense summer as an excuse, as October was well underway and college applications were starting to come due. Only Michael and Goff knew how badly this rattled me.

Then I got sick two weeks before Halloween. I didn't think much of it at first. I felt like I had a cold.

Michael felt my forehead. "You're not going to practice."

"It's just a cold," I said, knocking his hand away. "You know as well as I do that if it's upper respiratory and you feel like it, light exercise is all right."

"That's cute. Look me in the eye and tell me you feel like doing anything besides sleeping."

I sighed and looked him in the eye. I felt like death warmed over, and we both knew it. Light exercise? The only exercise I felt like right then was pulling my comforter back and crawling under it.

"Oh, Remy." Michael drew me into his arms. "I'm taking you home right after school. Then I'll bring the car back here for Geoff and catch a ride with someone else."

I nodded, and even that hurt. "I've got some Tylenol in my backpack. Maybe that plus a Rockstar will hold me together until school gets out."

Michael pulled out his phone and started texting.

"Geoff?" I said.

He nodded. "Just updating him. If you get worse, text me and I'll take you home right away."

"You'll miss class." I knew I should have protested more, but that would have taken more than I had in me right then.

"I'll take you by the office first. They'll take one look at you and I'll be excused."

I thought for a moment. Even that was sluggish. "Actually, Michael? Will you take me home now?"

"That's the first sensible thing you've said in weeks," Michael said.

We stopped by the office, and then I handed my boyfriend the keys. Michael probably didn't have a full driver's license, but I was in no shape to get myself home. I guess I fell asleep on the way, because the next thing I remembered was Michael gently shaking me awake. "We're here, sleeping beauty," he said, kissing my forehead. "Damn, you're burning up. Should I take you to the doctor, instead?"

"I'll see if I can get an appointment an' text you," I mumbled.

Michael shook his head. "Can you make it into the house and upstairs by yourself?"

Now that I'd given up, I didn't have to pretend. "Probably not."

Michael jumped out of the car and came around to open my door. After helping me out, he grabbed my bag and supported me as we went inside and up to my room.

He held me steady while I stripped out of my jeans and sweatshirt, admiring the view. "Ordinarily I'd love to take advantage of you in nothing but a T-shirt and your boxer briefs, but I don't think you're up for it."

"I could just lie there and let you have your way with me," I said, my voice muffled by my pillow as I all but collapsed into bed.

"I—damn, Remy. How much weight have you lost this fall?" I pried my eyes open to see concern all over my boyfriend's face.

"S'not weight, it's just bulk from not lifting."

"If you say so." Michael didn't look convinced, or even sound it. "I mean it. If you get a doctor's appointment, call or text me. Or Geoff. I'll let him know what's happening."

"Okay," I said, but I felt sleep closing in.

*

When I woke up, it was to my mother's gentle shaking. "Wake up, Jeremy. We need to change your sheets."

"Whaa—"

"You've got a fever, and you've soaked them clear through. Your T-shirt, too, sweetheart."

I sat up and immediately fell back down. "Dizzy, Mom."

"Take it more slowly this time," she said gently.

This time she helped me to sit up, holding me steady until I caught my bearings. Then she helped me out of bed and over to my desk chair. I slumped over onto my desk, resting. "I feel horrible."

"I don't doubt it for a moment, Jeremy, not with a fever like this one," she said, pulling my apparently soaked sheets off the bed.

Then Goff padded in, squinting against the light. "What's going on?"

"Geoffrey, your brother's sick. Would you go get him one of those sports drinks, but cut it in half with water?"

"Sure, Mom." He left, scratching his belly on the way out.

When Goff returned a short time later, Mom mostly had my bed remade. She handed me some Tylenol. "Take these, dear, and then drink as much of that sports drink as you can. You need to replace fluids and electrolytes in the worst way."

I sat at my desk, sipping watered-down sports drink and generally feeling miserable. "How'd you know?"

"Know what?" Mom said, sitting down on my bed, waiting for me to finish.

"To check on me."

She smiled. "You've caused quite a stir. Michael texted Geoffrey, who skipped practice to look in on you. A good thing, too, because this isn't the first set of sheets you've been through. You looked horrible, and he called me. This is the first time we've been able to rouse you. You've got a doctor's appointment in the morning. Urgent care's closed or I'd take you in right now. If you hadn't woken up or your fever hadn't broken, you'd probably be in the back of an ambulance at some point in time."

"Oh," I said, still listless. The fluids helped.

"Can you tell me what's wrong?" Mom looked worried.

I sighed. I had no energy. "Uh...fever. Fatigue, but you knew that. My throat's sore. I ache all over, and if I don't stop drinking this stuff, I'm going to puke it all back up." I shuddered, suddenly unable to stand the taste.

"Any bit you keep down will help, I'm sure. It sounds like flu to me, but I'm not a doctor," she said. "Geoffrey, can you bring the bathroom trashcan in here in case your brother throws up? It's bigger than the one in here."

"Sure, Mom."

Mom got up. "Why don't you try getting back in bed? Sleep can only help at this point. Then the rest of us can get back to sleep, as well."

"Sorry to get everyone up," I whispered, barely awake.

"Oh, sweetheart, you've nothing to apologize for," she said, kissing my forehead.

"Goodnight, Germy, I hope you feel better soon," I heard Goff say. It sounded like he was far, far away.

When I woke up again, it was morning. I lay still, taking stock. I felt only marginally better, but at least my fever was gone. Mostly. I felt wretched but had stopped sweating. So...progress?

I checked the time and obviously wasn't going to school since it was well past 10:00 a.m. Then I looked at my phone. Three texts from Michael, all of which were variations on "How are you? I'm really worried."

I texted him back.

REMY: *Rough night. Still feel horrible. MD later 2day?*

When I sat up, I still felt dizzy but nothing as bad as last night. I rested in place before trying to stand. After that, I hoisted myself up using my desk chair for support. I didn't even bother with clothing, wrapping myself in my robe.

"Jeremy, is that you?" Mom called.

Who else would it be? Goff was at school and Dad at work. "Yes, Mom."

"I was just about to get you up," she said, coming up the stairs. "You have a doctor's appointment in forty-five minutes. Are you hungry?"

I shuddered at the thought of eating anything. "No, but I'm going to shower."

"Are you sure that's wise? What if you fall down?"

"I feel gross. What if I sit on that plastic step stool from the kitchen?"

Mom nodded. "That'll work. I'll be right back."

I shuffled into the bathroom I shared with Goff and sat on the toilet to wait. Mom came back soon enough, and I turned on the recirculating pump to heat the water without running it all down the drain. California and its droughts. What can you do? I undressed myself while the water warmed up and then turned on the shower and its now-hot water.

It felt wonderful to sit under the water and let it run down me. I knew I didn't have a lot of time, but I needed to be clean. While I was in there, Mom set out fresh clothes for me, nothing fancy, just jeans, a tee, and a hoodie.

I checked myself out in the mirror. I really had lost weight. I could see ribs that had not been visible this summer. I knew I'd told Michael it was loss of bulk from not lifting, but I was worried. Maybe I was just dehydrated, I told myself, but deep down I knew that wasn't it.

I pocketed my phone and left my room. Mom waited outside. "Ready? We have just enough time to get to the doctor's. Your regular doctor was booked up, so you'll be seeing the nurse practitioner. I hope that's all right."

"It's fine." Like I had the energy to argue even if I objected.

Mom looked worried. "We can reschedule—"

"No, Mom, it's really fine. I'm just bushed."

Neither of us said much on the drive over, but I pulled out my phone and stared at the browser's search field. It was the last thing I wanted to do, but I made myself do it. I typed "HIV symptoms" and hit Enter.

Chapter Fifteen

"Well, Jeremy," the NP said. "You present a bit of a puzzle."

"Yay, me." I'd been out of bed for an hour, and it had been about forty minutes too long. I sagged against the exam table.

He smiled. "Most of your symptoms sound like the flu. That the fatigue has gone on so long concerns me, and that rash you say has just developed in the last twenty-four hours isn't a typical sign of the flu. Otherwise, everything else sounds like classic flu symptoms. It's a bit early for the flu, but it's not unheard of."

The NP pulled a tube with a swab sealed in it out of a drawer. "I'm going to swab you for the flu to see if indeed you have it, but in the meantime, we'll go ahead and treat you as if you've got it." He broke the seal. "What I need you to do now is tip your head back and try not to sneeze. This isn't going to be particularly comfortable."

With that, the NP stuck the biggest cotton swab I'd ever seen all the way up my nose. I swore I felt it against the back of my eyes. "What the hell?"

"I'm sorry," he said, quickly resealing the swab in its test tube. "There's no way to warn anyone. As I said, we'll treat this as if it were the flu, and that means plenty of rest, fluids, and Tylenol to help keep the fever and aches under control. You can gargle with saltwater for your throat or use cough drops. Some people recommend a teaspoon of honey in a cup of warm water, so you might try that, as well. Since we've caught this within a day, there'll be a prescription for Tamiflu at the pharmacy within fifteen minutes for you. Stomach upset, even vomiting, can be associated with the flu, so if that continues to be a problem, call, because there are antiemetics that can be prescribed. As for the rash, it may just be contact dermatitis due to your fever sweats. If it gets worse, try some cortisone cream, one of the ones with colloidal oatmeal in it since that's good for the skin. It's over the counter, so you won't need a prescription."

I felt his eyes linger on me as I noticed a discreet red ribbon pin on his name badge. His name was Heath Nichols. "Jeremy... I'm concerned about the long-lasting fatigue, the weight loss, and the rash. Combined with your other symptoms, they point to other illnesses."

I looked at the floor. Thanks to my reading on the way there, I knew exactly what he meant, and I couldn't cope with it, not right then.

But he plowed on. "I noticed in your chart that no one seems to have talked to you about your sexual health. That's a major oversight for a man your age."

"My coach has," I mumbled.

"That's good," the nurse practitioner said, "very good, but is there a chance, no matter how small, that this could be something else? Maybe you've had some encounters, even just one, where you might not have been careful?"

I couldn't say anything, like my mouth had been welded shut. I knew the answer, and by my silence, I was pretty sure he did too.

He helped me sit back up on the exam table and then put his arm around my shoulder. I didn't feel like he was a creeper or anything. "The other thing this looks like to me is acute retroviral syndrome, or ARS, the first, early stages of infection with HIV."

I only stared at the floor. "I know," I whispered. "I looked up the symptoms."

"Have you been tested?"

I shook my head.

"Can I order a test for you?"

"I can't... Not right now. I mean, my parents..."

"Under the law, there is strict confidentiality in matters of sexual health to protect people over the age of fourteen," the NP said. "Your parents have no right to see the results or even know what you're being tested for."

"If I start seeing an AIDS specialist, that'll pretty much let the cat out of the bag." My eyes welled up with tears. "I just can't face this right now."

He nodded. "I'll be right back."

When he returned, the NP handed me his card. "This has my e-mail address and direct line. Enter this in your phone so you don't have to worry about anyone finding it or asking you questions you're not ready to answer. I want you to think about this, and when you're ready, contact me and I'll give you resources outside the HMO about free and low-cost testing. At least you'll know."

I sniffled. "Okay."

"Just promise me one thing."

I looked up.

"Don't go alone. Bring someone with you, both when you go the first time and when you get your results."

I nodded. "I can do that."

"I'm going to put in one last pitch for a test today," he said. "If I'm right and this is ARS, the sooner you're on medication, the easier it will be to control and the sooner you'll go back to leading a perfectly normal life. Did you catch that last bit? A normal life—sports, dating, and everything else."

I only shook my head.

"I understand—"

"How can you? My life is over, and I'm not even eighteen," I said thickly. "Two months of crappy decisions, and I'll pay for it forever."

"Because I've been poz for eight years."

My mouth fell open.

"I do triathlons. I'm active in the community. My husband and I have been together for six years, married for four," Heath said. "I think I get it."

Something did not add up. "Wait...you've had it for eight years, but you met your husband after that?"

"Life doesn't end with a diagnosis, Jeremy." Heath almost looked amused, and that didn't make sense either. "In my case it started. I knew I had to get my act together and get healthy."

My head spun from too much information and input. "Can I... I just need to get through this, and then I'll get tested, I promise."

"Can I hold you to that?" Heath smiled when he said it.

"I'll tell my boyfriend what you said. He'll never let me wriggle out of it," I said.

"He'll need to know, too, you know."

I smiled—or tried. "We got together after my slutty phase."

"See? You know what I'm talking about, but can we not use the term 'slutty'? You'll experience enough criticism without attaching moral terms to sex."

I nodded. "As soon as I kick this, I'll e-mail you for information."

"I hope so," Heath said. "Don't forget to stop by the pharmacy."

*

I shook off the flu or the ARS or whatever it was but never felt back to my normal self. I still had applications to submit and schoolwork to attend to, so a prolonged convalescence was not a luxury I allowed myself. Crew, however, continued to suffer from whatever was wrong with me.

Whatever. I knew. I didn't want to say it aloud, but I knew.

The Saturday after I had gotten so sick, Michael and I were hanging out in the backyard. He had already endured practice. I'd ridden in the launch since rowing required more energy than I had to give it at that point. School, I managed, but rowing, no. Fortunately, October was basically summer lite in the Sacramento Valley, beautiful weather without hideous temperatures.

I still wore jeans and a hoodie. I never seemed to warm up.

"I'm glad you're doing better," he said softly. He took my hand. "You scared the hell out of me."

"I scared me too."

"So, what'd the doctor say?"

I smiled, thinking about Heath. "I saw a nurse practitioner. He said he'd treat it like the flu, although the culture came back negative." I said nothing for a moment. I looked around to make sure neither parent was in earshot. I think Dad was watching Goff's football practice or something manly like that. I couldn't see Mom, but that didn't mean anything. "He said the other possibility was something called ARS—acute retrovirus syndrome."

Michael looked at me blankly. "Which is...?"

"HIV is a retrovirus."

His mouth formed a silent O of surprise. Then, "Did you get tested?"

I shook my head. "I couldn't face it right then."

"You need to."

"Of course, I do," I said, rolling my eyes. "I just... Not then."

He opened his mouth, presumably to launch into an impassioned argument about why. I knew why, but that did not mean I was prepared for the test results.

"Michael, stop. I never said I wasn't going to get tested. I said I couldn't face it right then. I could barely stand upright. Getting tested for a life-changing disease? Give me a break."

He looked at me strangely. "You didn't say life-threatening."

"Huh. You're right." I thought about that. "I talked about it with the nurse practitioner. He must've reached me more than I thought. He's poz. From what he said, his life actually improved after he found out."

"That's bizarre."

I shrugged. I was the last one to judge. "I guess it made him take charge and clean up his act or something. He's into triathlons and get this: he met his husband years after the diagnosis."

"Wow. That's kind of cool if you think about it," Michael said.

"It certainly gave me something to think about, like maybe it's not the life-ending disaster I'd been building up for."

"Maybe not, but it's still not what I would've chosen for you," he said quietly.

"Me neither." I sighed. However, it was the life I had ended up choosing for myself anyway, and didn't that just suck?

"So, what're you going to do?"

"Get tested, obviously." I thought for minute. "Will you go with me?"

"Of course, I will. Like you even have to ask?" Michael looked hurt.

I wrapped my arms around myself, telling myself I was cold and not scared. "I didn't want to assume..."

Michael launched himself at me. "Start assuming." He moved me around until we were both on the same lounger, kind of like on that roof that night in San Diego. So much had happened since last April. "So, when do we do this?"

"I'll e-mail Heath and get some info—"

"Who," Michael said, "is Heath?"

"The nurse practitioner," I said. "This new jealous streak of yours is kind of cute, yet disturbing."

"I'm not jealous."

I smiled. "Of course, you're not."

"I'm not," Michael protested, pulling me onto his lap. It was not so much his lap as it was me leaning back against him, like spooning, only we were sitting up. "I just want to know who this guy is who's somehow managed to give you even a little bit of hope."

"I told you. He was the nurse practitioner I saw. Anyway, he told me when I was ready, he'd send me info about testing at the free clinic so I don't have to tell my doctor right away."

"You'll have to tell her sooner or later, won't you?" Michael said softly. "Preferably sooner."

"Yes, but baby steps. This is a lot for me to wrap my mind around." I relaxed back into Michael. He felt good. I felt moderately horrible. I knew I should have been worried about my mom finding us like that, but it struck me as one more thing I didn't have the energy for.

"So, how will we explain your absence from school?" Michael asked a few minutes later.

"Or yours." I thought for a minute. "It'll be a medical office. I'll get a note."

"Or I'll tell Lodestone what's going on and take you after school. He's not going to mind if I miss one practice."

The thought of telling Lodestone... "You can't miss practice. I'll go by myself."

"The hell you will." Michael sounded fierce. "I'm not letting you face this alone, and I wouldn't even if you weren't my boyfriend."

"Am I?" I said. "Your boyfriend, I mean?"

Michael kissed the back of my neck. It made my skin crawl in an entirely good way. I shuddered. He had to know what it did to me. "I am absolutely, positively, one hundred percent your boyfriend. I thought you knew that."

"I'm not really very secure these days, and we've never actually talked about it," I mumbled.

I felt him nod behind me. "True enough, but we've done a lot about it."

"I told Heath you were my boyfriend."

Michael growled. "Good."

I laughed. "He's too old for me. I like my men younger."

"I'll keep that in mind."

I pulled his arms around me. "I'll get the information on where to go, and then..."

"Yes?"

The entire idea terrified me, but if indeed I had HIV, Lodestone would know soon enough. "Are you sure you don't mind skipping practice?"

"I wouldn't have brought it up if I hadn't meant it," Michael said.

I could get used to someone who said exactly what he meant. "Who knows, maybe there'll be Saturday hours, and we won't have to miss practice or school."

*

Waiting for the results was the most nerve-racking thing I have ever done, harder even than walking up the steps to the clinic in the first place. Fortunately, the clinic indeed had Saturday hours, and there was one not too far from the port in West Sacramento, so I avoided Davis entirely. Michael stood by me the entire time. Unfortunately, he couldn't graft himself to my side, so I endured the waiting alone. Well, not entirely alone. Goff knew I'd gotten tested, but if our parents knew anything was up, they remained oddly silent.

"Germy, you've got to tell them." He sat at the end of my bed where I had curled up under the comforter because I—as usual—couldn't stay warm.

"Tell them what? That I spent my summer as a manwhore?" I said. "There's nothing to tell them yet."

Goff made a disgusted noise. "That's bullshit, and you know it. You're sick. Just look at yourself. This isn't a cold or the flu, this is serious. They're not the enemy."

I sighed. "You keep telling me that, but as I keep telling you, we've had different experiences with them."

"And you won't tell me what that means. I hate that."

"I don't want to ruin your view of Mom and Dad." I didn't, but it was true. I'd overheard them on more than one occasion, and it didn't make me feel good. I knew when it came out in the open it would be ugly. Why couldn't they have just kept their mouths shut, or at least made sure they were alone in the house? "I don't want to argue about this anymore. I have my reasons, and you're just going to have to accept that."

"Yeah, whatever." Neither of us said anything for a while. "So, when do you find out?"

"I'm supposed to call in and a recording will tell me if my results are ready."

Goff looked surprised. "They don't tell you on the phone?"

"Nope." I shook my head. "They don't want anyone doing anything stupid if the results are positive."

"You'd think they'd at least tell you if you were negative."

I had to laugh. "Yeah, but if they did that and you got a recording, then you'd know you were positive and still might do something stupid, right? They've been doing this since the '80s, so they've figured out all the tricks."

"I guess. I just hate waiting. It's like I'm nervous for you or something," Goff said.

"Of all of us, I think I want to know the least," I muttered.

Goff gave me a knowing look. "Is that because you know the answer?"

"Probably. Anyway, to answer your question, I call in tomorrow." I sounded calm, but the reality was that my stomach had wrapped itself around my spine, I was so wrecked about it. Thinking I knew the answer and receiving confirmation were two entirely different things. So, spending the day at school tomorrow while waiting to call in would probably have me puking up breakfast or something. I also knew I'd skip the rest of the day when the clinic told me to come in.

"You'd tell me, right?" Goff said. "If you were poz?"

"Of course." I gave him a pained look, even though I knew full well that if the results went the way I thought they would, I would have to take the time to process it. "You're my brother. Besides, I'd need your help to break it to Mom and Dad."

Goff looked relieved, and I let him steer the conversation in other directions. There was only so long I could contemplate my mortality anyway.

While we talked, I texted Michael.

REMY: *I call in tomorrow.*

MICHAEL: *Like I could forget? Let me know ASAP?*

REMY: *All they tell me is whether or not 2 come in.*

MICHAEL: *Yeah, but I know U. U'll drive there ASAP.*

REMY: *Guilty and yes.*

MICHAEL: *I'll go with.*

REMY: *xoxo*

"Mikey?" Goff said.

"He goes by Michael now, but yes."

Goff snorted. "We've known him since what? Fourth grade?"

"About that, yes. Let's just say he was very persuasive when he told me to call him Michael." I smiled at the memory.

"Is there a story there?"

I turned red. "Not that I'm going to tell you."

Then I yawned.

Goff looked at his watch. "Okay, time for bed."

"It's eight thirty."

"So? I didn't say it was time for me to go to bed," Goff said.

I replied in the appropriate manner. I threw a pillow at him. "I'm not an invalid."

"No, but you're not at full strength either," he said.

There wasn't anything I could say to that, so I got out of bed and immediately started shivering. Goff looked at me as if to say, *See?*

"All right, all right, I'll go to bed."

*

I sat in my car with my head against the headrest, eyes closed.

"Talk to me, Remy. Don't shut me out."

I had called in as soon as lunch started. The recording told me my results were ready. I guess it wasn't technically a recording, more like a computer-generated response, since no one had used actual tape recorders during my lifetime so far as I knew. If they had, I wonder how the clinic would have updated it for each client's results—

It took a conscious effort to halt the mental freefall.

"What do you want me to say?" I said, not opening my eyes.

"I don't know, just tell me what's going on in that complicated mind of yours," Michael said. "Silence can't be good."

I sighed. "I don't know which is worse, suspecting or knowing for sure." I opened my eyes and looked at him. "Actually, I do. It was the look of pity in the counselor's eyes."

"I think she was just sorry to deliver news like that to someone still in high school," Michael said.

"Yeah, but I don't look like I'm in high school." I thought for a moment. "It occurs to me that's part of what landed me in trouble in the first place."

Michael put his hand on my knee. "So, what do you want to do now?"

"I have no idea. Saying 'Go to Disneyland' is so trite, don't you think?"

"At least your sense of humor—such as it is—is intact." He shook his head.

"Gallows humor may be the only thing that gets me through this," I snapped.

"Easy there, tiger, I'm on your side," he said. "And honestly, antiretrovirals are the only things that will get you through this, so suck this up and listen. You need to tell your parents and get on medication. Now."

"Don't you think I know that?"

Michael gave me a bland look. "I know you do, but that doesn't mean you're going to do it. You need careful management, Remy. I've learned that much about you."

"Don't patronize me!"

Goddamn, where did he get off saying shit like that? I'd just been dealt a diagnosis of death, and he's telling me I need to be led about like a child?

"I'm not patronizing you, Remy. I'm stating a fact. If you know you need to do one thing, you're just as likely to do its opposite." He reached over and took my chin in his hand, turning my face toward his. He kissed me lightly. I didn't kiss him back. "I want you around for a long, long time. You need to talk to your doctor. I don't know anything about treating HIV, but I'm willing to bet your doctor does, just as I'm willing to bet it involves medication."

I didn't say anything, but I'd noticed we had not kissed on the lips as much since I'd gotten so sick with what we both knew was ARS.

"I know I need to, okay? That doesn't make it any easier."

"I know," he said softly.

I refrained from screaming "how" or anything like that. He meant well, and he had cut class—again—to help me.

"Besides," Michael continued, "you can't row, not at the levels you want to, if you keep losing muscle mass and strength."

Of course, he chose that line of reasoning. "You fight dirty."

"Is there some other way to fight?"

I laughed. I had to. "Asshole."

He smiled. "But hopefully I'm your asshole."

"For as long as you'll have me." I might have been temporarily upset, but I knew when I had it good.

"Then that's all that matters. But you know you don't have to do this alone. Geoff and I will be with you when you tell your parents."

I made a face. "Ugh, that means coming out to them at the same time."

"Well, yes, unless you want to tell them you use IV drugs, which I don't think you do," he said. "Keep in mind, this likely means coming out to my parents sooner than I'm ready to as well, and before you say anything, I do realize it will be far less traumatic for me."

"At least you admit that much," I grumbled, but far more good-naturedly than before.

"I'm younger than you are," he said dryly, "but that doesn't make me dumber. So, how do you want to spend the rest of the afternoon?"

"Oh, I don't know. Cutting class is only a thrill if you're having fun, and this? This ain't it. Take me home, I guess? I don't think I feel like going to practice. I may just veg out and watch television."

"That sounds fine." Michael got out of the car.

"What're you doing? You make no sense."

Then he stood at my door. "I'm driving. You're distracted, and I want to live."

"Yeah, okay. That works." Then I thought of something. "Let's hit the store. I want ice cream."

"Sure, why not?" Michael laughed. "You could use the calories, and one day won't destroy my training."

"You're staying with me?" For some reason that made me feel more hopeful than I had for a while.

Michael smiled. "I'm not leaving you alone."

"I'm paying but get your own flavors. I'm not sharing."

"That's my Remy."

Chapter Sixteen

MICHAEL: *What the hell's going on?*

GEOFF: *Laurel says he collapsed in the middle of O-chem lab.*

MICHAEL: *Shit.*

GEOFF: *Yep. She said he looked bad, real pale but kind of red. Cold 2 & confused about lab. Next thing she knew he was on the floor.*

MICHAEL: *Where R U now?*

GEOFF: *Ambulance. EMTs giving him fluids. Say his pulse&breathing R really rapid.*

MICHAEL: *See U at...*

GEOFF: *Sutter Davis [sends contacts] Can you keep trying my parents? Dad's seeing patients and who knows where Mom is? She's on the road a lot.*

MICHAEL: *Will do.*

*

"Young man!" someone called after him, but Michael ignored her. He had to find Geoff and the critical-care ICU. He caught an elevator going up just before the doors closed. When the doors opened, he took off again. He skidded to a halt in front of a nurses' station.

"Where's the fire?" an older woman asked.

He looked at her tag. Nurse supervisor. "I'm sorry, ma'am. I'm here to see Remy Babcock. He was brought in earlier this afternoon. I was told he was in this ICU."

She flipped through the inventory of who was on the ward. "Do you mean Jeremy Babcock? He's in room 8A, but I have to warn you. He's not conscious right now. He's also scheduled for tests and might not even be there."

"That's all right. I'll take my chances. Besides, his brother's here, and I'll talk to him if Remy's not there," Michael said.

"I'll buzz you in," the nurse supervisor said.

Once inside, Michael quickly found 8A. He knocked on the glass door.

"Hey, Michael. Come in," Geoff said.

Michael claimed the other seat in the bay, a stool. "Sorry I couldn't get here sooner. If I cut class anymore, I'll be on probation for crew. Lodestone's been really patient, but he said enough's enough. How is he?"

Geoff gestured to Remy. He lay on a typical hospital bed, his trunk elevated, hooked into supportive apparatuses, not just an oxygen feed but an actual mask, as well as more of the IV fluids Geoff had mentioned and another bag that could only be the antibiotics. Vancomycin, the label read. None of it made much sense, but it all looked frightening.

"Wow."

"Yep. Any luck reaching my parents?"

Michael nodded. "I actually spoke to your mom. After she chewed me out for interrupting her, she thanked me for calling. She was in the South Bay, but she said she'd be here as soon as she could. But your dad's receptionist? I don't like him."

"No kidding," Geoff said. "I don't know why 'My brother's on the way to the hospital by ambulance' doesn't count as an emergency, but Dad needs to talk to that jerk."

"Unless those're your dad's orders," Michael said.

"Remy's always had a different relationship with them than I have," Geoff said, looking troubled. "I'll worry about that later."

"Right, we've got bigger issues."

Geoff met Michael's eyes. "Like, what are we going to tell my parents?"

"Did he ever tell your parents about his test results?" Michael ran a hand through his hair.

"No."

"That's just great." Michael shook his head. "I know he was having a lot of problems facing it himself, not that I blame him, but he's just dumped it in our laps."

"Our?" Geoff said.

"Yes, *our*. I'm not leaving this all to you, even if it scares the hell out of me. I'm still his boyfriend." Michael thought for a moment. "Unless you're kicking me out."

"Oh God no. No way, Michael. You don't know what you mean to Remy," Geoff said. "Or what it's meant to me not to be the only one who knows about any of this."

"Knows what, boys?" Dina Babcock said.

"Crap," Michael said, turning to face the curtain-covered glass wall.

Geoff stood up. "Hi, Mom."

"Hello, Geoffrey. Michael. Now someone needs to start explaining, because one of my children is lying in the ICU and I'm about sixty seconds away from hysteria." She looked around. "Where's your father?"

"I'm sorry, Mrs. Babcock. I left him a message, but I couldn't get through to him," Michael said.

"Same here, Mom." Geoff sighed.

"Let me guess. His receptionist. I'm so sick of that man," Dina said. "Now. Start. Talking."

Michael and Geoff looked at each other. "So far, it's looking like sepsis, some kind of blood poisoning?" Geoff said. "The doctors are running tests—"

"How does a healthy seventeen-year-old boy get sepsis?" Dina demanded.

"We'll get to that in a moment," Michael said. "Geoff's telling you what he knows, which is all I know. Other than tests, he's on fluids to keep him hydrated, plus antibiotics."

Dina looked at the IVs. "Vancomycin? Damn. That's one of the most powerful antibiotics around. They must be scared." She looked to Geoff and Michael. "There's still something you're not telling me, isn't there?"

"Mom, this isn't really the time—"

"Oh no, this is exactly the time—"

"The time for what? And why am I always the last to know?"

Geoff sighed. "Hi, Dad."

"Thanks for joining us, Steven," Dina said. "You'd know more if that creep who answers your phones listened to your son and his friend when they called you with emergencies."

"Dina, that's not fair. Just because you're in sales and can dash off from lunch with doctors at some high-priced club doesn't mean I can. I was in the middle of a patient—"

"Yes, well, it looks like your son's a patient, too, and you're the last to know because there's no way to reach you," Dina said flatly.

"Why don't I see if I can find a doctor who can tell you what's going on?" Michael said and slipped out of the bay before anyone could say anything.

He returned momentarily with one of the ICU's physicians.

"I was just coming to talk to you. I'm glad you're all here."

"Why's he here?" Steven said, indicating Michael. "I get that you're a friend of Remy's—"

"Dad," Geoff said.

Dina sighed. "He's here because Remy would want him here, and because he knows more than he and Geoff are letting on right now."

"It's rather crowded, and there are more of you than there should be," the physician said. "There's an unused bay down the hall. We'll talk there."

She led them to the empty patient room and then shoved the bed over. When everyone was seated, she started talking. "First the good news: your son has sepsis—"

"That's good news?" Steven said.

"It's better than septic shock," the physician said coolly. "It means a massive infection has triggered a body-wide immune response but Jeremy has not yet suffered any organ failure. So, while there is systemic inflammation, which is not a good thing, he won't be facing the more extreme complications. We caught it before the inflammation got too far out of hand, which means his body didn't have enough time to form little blood clots that might've blocked the flow of blood to his extremities or his brain. So, no gangrene in his fingers and toes or loss of cognitive functions.

"All of that said, this is a very serious condition, and he's nowhere near out of the woods. What concerns me is that he appears to have a very compromised immune system. Is your son HIV-positive? Because that makes a difference in terms of treatment. Ordinarily, he'd already be on Prednisone to knock out the inflammation, but Pred is a powerful immunosuppressive drug. For obvious reasons I don't want to give it to someone whose immune system is already failing."

"Boys?" Dina said.

Michael and Geoff looked at each other hopelessly. "He was going to tell them," Michael said. He hated to break Remy's confidence, but damn, his life was on the line.

"He was also stalling," Geoff said.

"Because he didn't feel comfortable, and you know it," Michael said.

"Damn it, didn't feel comfortable telling us *what*?" Steven yelled. "This is his life you're dithering over."

Geoff took a deep breath. "Okay, you're not going to like it, and don't you dare yell at me or Michael because we had nothing to do with it, but yes, he's poz."

"What?" Steven screamed. "How the hell could you keep something like this secret?"

"Because of this," Michael said, looking around the room, "and it was Remy's job to tell you because it's his life. I'm out of here. Good luck with your family melodrama. I'll talk to you later, Geoff."

"Thank you," Remy's doctor said. "That makes a huge difference in his treatment. I'll bring an HIV specialist in immediately."

Dina followed him out into the hall. "Michael, wait. I'm sorry for my husband's behavior. Obviously, we're shocked, and just as obviously there's more to this story. Are...are you okay?"

"Thank you, Mrs. Babcock." Michael took a steadying breath. "I'm fine, perfectly healthy, and yes, there's a whole lot you don't know that will be coming out soon. As it were. This happened...before Remy and I got together."

"So, you and Remy..."

"Yes, he's my boyfriend. I'm sorry you had to find out this way, but he really did intend to tell you. I hope you can understand how hard this has been for him to deal with, and I think I understand why. Now maybe Geoff will understand too."

"I'll deal with Remy's father, and Remy's right. He and the boys' father have always had a more difficult relationship. Geoff's never wanted to see it, but... Well, no sense in airing dirty linens in a public hallway. You'll find it all out eventually. Thank you for being there for my son. If you're in any trouble for missing school or practice, I'll talk to your parents."

"Thanks, Mrs. Babcock, that would be great. I've missed a bit of school, yeah. Coach Lodestone's been great about all of this, but I'm at the end of line with him too," Michael said.

Dina nodded. "Go ahead and send your parents' contacts to my cell phone. I'll be here for a while, but it's not looking like Jeremy will be waking up anytime soon."

"I'll do that before I bike home, but right now I think I need not to be here."

"Yes, sometimes Steven has that effect on people, but don't let him run you off," Dina said. "Jeremy needs you, and so does Geoff. Do you know how to reach Geoff's girlfriend?"

Michael nodded. "I'll call her once I'm outside of the hospital."

*

"I can't believe my son did that," Steven said, disbelief as plain in his voice as the nose on his face. "Not Remy."

Dina met Michael's eyes and shook her head.

"Well, Dad, he's got the HIV status to prove it, so I'm not sure where you're coming from," Geoff said.

They met in the Babcocks' living room. Michael's parents had offered to come with, but he had assured them that he'd be fine, that Remy's mother would watch out for him. Dina had spoken to them, assuring Michael's parents that her husband was stunned but not hostile. Dina had ended up speaking to Michael's mother in particular about having a gay son. As Michael had predicted, his parents had not known, per se, that he was gay, but were not surprised either.

"I still think this conversation needs to wait until Remy's well enough to participate in it," Michael said. Despite Mrs. Babcock's assurances, he would put nothing past Mr. Babcock. Between what Remy had told him, plus his own observations, the man struck him as the sort to use bluster to make up for being parentally AWOL.

"I'm not sure Remy has that much time," Steven said. "He needs to start treatment."

"But how does invading his privacy help that?" Dina said.

"His privacy is what allowed this to flourish under our noses, Dina. I don't think he gets to have any privacy for a while."

Michael coughed. "If I may, Mr. Babcock, what allowed this to happen was being closeted and not feeling like he could be open. The stress of the closet cuts you off from the support of friends and family, your whole life, really. I was lucky I was never really in the closet. Remy wasn't so fortunate."

"I'm sure it's not that bad," Steven said, justifying in Michael's mind everything Remy had ever told him.

"Dad!" Geoff said.

"Are you gay, Mr. Babcock? Do you have many gay or lesbian patients?" Michael knew he had to be strong for Remy, so he stared Mr. Babcock right in the eyes. When Steven didn't reply, he said, "Are you? Do you?"

"I don't like your attitude, young man."

"I can live with that," Michael said. "Can Remy?"

Geoff snickered.

"I don't see what that has to do with anything. This isn't about me," Steven said. "I'm a therapist, so I can set my personal feelings aside."

"Just answer his question, Steven," Dina said. "You're being deliberately obtuse, and you know it. In any event, this is your personal life and not your practice, so don't pull that 'I'm a mental health professional' garbage."

Michael and Steven continued their stare for dominance, and it was not Michael who backed down. "All right, fine. It's different when it's your son. Are you happy, now?"

"No, I'm not. My boyfriend is in the ICU because he made a lot of risky decisions this summer. Those are on him, but part of that was because he didn't feel safe coming out," Michael said. "So not only am I not happy, I don't really like you a whole lot if this is what Remy faced."

"You don't have to like me. You just have to respect me as your *boyfriend's* father."

"Respect is earned, Mr. Babcock," Michael said, his pulse racing, understanding Remy more and more if this was what his father was like. "Now, as far as what happened, what I do know is that he met someone at the boathouse—"

"The boathouse! I'll sue those bastards into the ground. I'll make sure Lodestone never coaches anywhere again—"

"This had nothing to do with the junior crew, and when Coach Lodestone found out about it, he went nuclear. I watched the fight, and it almost turned physical," Michael said tightly. "It was someone involved in one of the masters programs. I think Lodestone turned the guy in to USRowing, so his coaching career is over. As

I understand it, the police investigation is ongoing, but from what Remy's told me, the laws in this state covering statutory rape are complicated by 'Romeo and Juliet' clauses and made even murkier when the people involved are the same gender. So, go right ahead and sue, but Cap City's followed the letter of the law and the rules of USRowing."

"Sounds to me like you're still trying to dodge any responsibility for letting Remy down, Dad," Geoff said. Michael looked at him gratefully.

"Go to your room," Steven said. All Michael could do was shake his head.

"That'll make it hard for him to tell you what he knows, Steven," Dina said.

Steven swore. "I wish I'd never heard any of this."

"How'll that help Remy?" Michael said. "Anyway, he branched out and started meeting people online, and before you ask, I don't know. He never gave me the details beyond Grindr."

When Steven and Dina made noises of disgust, Michael said, "For what it's worth, I felt the same way."

"I...uh, encouraged him to delete all that after Nationals," Geoff said.

"That's something, at least," Dina said.

"Why?" Steven demanded. "That could be evidence."

Geoff rolled his eyes. "He lied about his age, Dad, which is how minors get around those things. And he deleted it because one of the guys he met went nuts with jealousy because I happened to be in the same room when they were talking on Skype—just talking, before you get any sick ideas. He didn't believe we were twins."

"That's about when Remy and I started dating," Michael said.

"Yeah?" Geoff said. "I was wondering how you wore him down."

Michael smiled. "Pretty much that was it, although we started at the Crew Classic."

"What the hell is going on with that crew? Boys hooking up? I'm taking this to the board," Steven said angrily.

"Why, because they're boys? That's a little homophobic," Geoff said. "Boys and girls hook up all the time, and nobody has a problem with that."

"And we're not the only gay kids on the crew," Michael said. "After all, other guys on the team were jealous, or so we were told. Take it to the board, and you'll sound like the raging homophobe you look like from here."

"What!" Steven roared. "I think it's time you went home, young man."

Michael stood up. "I've told you what I know. I'm not sure what good it did."

"I'll see you out." Geoff jumped up to follow him. On the front porch, he said, "Please don't judge him too harshly. He's just shocked."

"Whatever, man. He's your father. Hopefully, he gets over it before Remy comes home." Michael was pissed.

Geoff sighed. "Mom'll manage him. She always does."

"If this is what he's like, I think I understand why Remy was so reluctant to say anything. Anyway, keep me posted?"

"I will," Geoff said, "and thanks."

Chapter Seventeen

"Good, you're awake," said an affable voice.

I frowned, blinking against the bright light. "I...am, yes. Where am I?"

"You're in the intensive care unit at Sutter Hospital," an older man in a doctor's white coat said. "I'm Dr. Kravitz, your HIV specialist. I took over your care from the intensivist once your status came to light."

I closed my eyes again. Maybe all this would prove to be an elaborate nightmare. "Can you tell me what happened? Last thing I remember... I don't remember the last thing."

Dr. Kravitz snorted. "I'm not surprised. You were a very sick young man when you arrived. Your brother was terrified, and the other young man wasn't far behind. Is he your boyfriend?"

Oh crap. Had I been babbling or something? "No, he's just—"

"You don't need to hide anything from me, Mr. Babcock," Dr. Kravitz said with a low chuckle. "I've seen it all where this disease is concerned, believe me."

"What disease?" HIV was the last thing I wanted to discuss with a doctor or anyone else.

Dr. Kravitz set his chart down and gave me a look that made me squirm. "Don't play stupid with me. I've fought this disease since the beginning, and I've seen more young men die than anyone should. I was in residency at UC San Francisco in the early '80s when gay men started dying from some mysterious plague that no one could name. They called it GRID—gay-related immune deficiency. In 1984, we discovered it was caused by a retrovirus. It wasn't called HIV until 1986, long after I'd lost too many patients." He gave me a piercing look, like he was angry, even furious. Not at me, but at the disease. "Some people gave up hope, so I decided to specialize in the treatment of men like you. I still do. You're HIV positive. Your brother and your boyfriend told my colleagues when you were brought in with blood poisoning. They saved your life."

I frowned. "What do you mean?"

"What do I mean? It made a big difference in the drugs we used to treat you, to say nothing of getting you started on treatment for HIV itself, that's what I mean."

Son of a bitch. They told. I hardly knew what to think. That meant... "My parents know, don't they?"

He nodded. "They'd have found out eventually."

I fell back against my bed, my mind a whirl. My parents were going to freak, had already freaked. But they would have kittens all over again the next time I saw them.

"I can't deal with this, any of this."

"And why not? This is a good thing," Dr. Kravitz said, looking up from his charting again.

I made a face. "I don't want to deal with a daily cocktail of drugs, for one thing."

"You already are." Dr. Kravitz laughed. "Why do you think you're doing so well? Seriously, Jeremy, refusing to do this basic thing to take care of yourself is cutting off your nose to spite your face. The drugs available now, they can reduce your viral load—the detectable level of the virus in your body—essentially to zero. You'll still have to be careful if you bleed in public, you'll have to be safe with your sexual partners and inform them, but you'll lead a normal life. You'll learn to take care of yourself, to follow the schedule you'll need for your meds, but this will quickly become second nature."

"I don't want to do this." I crossed my arms. I knew I was being childish, but I couldn't stop the words from tumbling out.

"You already are. We're pumping them into your IV. Before you're released, you'll learn to take care of it yourself." Dr. Kravitz patted my hand. "Let me put it this way. Learning to do it yourself is a condition of your release. Now, as far as what else you can expect, you're still sick from the septicemia and you'll be on the antibiotics for a while longer. You'll be shaking that off faster and faster, however. Now that you're awake, you'll find your energy coming back quickly."

As much as I couldn't cope with the idea of HIV, I wanted out of the hospital. "Good. I can't really afford to miss more school. Or more crew."

"It'll take a little longer to build your strength for sports back up, but it'll come back fast. Taking care of the HIV will help with that too."

"I really am going to have to deal with this, aren't I?" I said.

"Only if you want to live." He looked at me over his glasses.

"That was blunt."

Dr. Kravitz shrugged. "I don't have time to hold your hand. Neither do you. You have a life to live. One of the HIV educators will be by later today or tomorrow to get started with you and tell you about the classes we have about managing a chronic disease. You'll talk about the condition itself, taking care of yourself, sexual health, notifying past partners, all kinds of things."

I nodded, suddenly exhausted by it all. I had a lot to learn and maybe not much time to learn it.

*

The HIV education specialist assigned to me turned out to be majorly cool and helped set my mind at ease. It did not hurt that he wasn't more than ten years older than I was. He hadn't been a manwhore like I'd been, but he understood the need, the sexual drive, and didn't judge. I would receive enough of that from my family, and he understood that too. They were holding back until I was stronger, but I knew it was only a matter of time.

In the meantime, I was moved from the ICU to a regular room and started working on missed assignments brought to me by Goff, Michael, and Laurel. My parents visited every day. Dad struggled with me and what happened, I could tell. Mom did, too, but not nearly as much. Then again, Mom and I always had gotten on better than Dad and I. Eventually I was cleared to go home. I still did not feel entirely normal, but my doctors told me I wouldn't, not with the septicemia, not for quite a while. I would have weekly appointments with Dr. Kravitz and the HIV educator for some time to come, but I was okay with that.

I went home in early November, so yeah, this year the Babcock and Castelreigh households had something to be thankful for. I, however, was just thankful that the two families decided not to share the holiday meal, because all hell broke loose at my house. So much for circling the wagons. I mean, when Cisco died, they were right there for me, but now, when I had a manageable disease? There was a circle, all right, a circular firing squad, and I was right in the middle.

"Remy," Dad said, sighing, "I still don't understand how you could do something like this."

And with that, my appetite, a sometime thing at the best of times, vanished. "Do we have to talk about this right now?"

"Yes, I think we do. Was this some kind of a suicide attempt? Gay kids are far more likely to attempt suicide, something on the order of two or three times more likely," Dad said.

I could only stare at my dad and blink. That was... unbelievable.

"Well?" Dad said. "I think it's a legitimate question. Was this some kind of slo-mo suicide attempt?"

"Yes, Dad. You got me. That's how I decided to kill myself to escape the existential agony and irony of suburban life—by banging as many men as possible," I said flatly. Suffering Christ, where the hell did he dig this garbage up? "In this case, it was in the neighborhood of eight or ten. You can just call me the he-whore of Babylon."

"Damn it, Jeremy, I'm just trying to understand— you, what you did, all of it. You don't have to be so sarcastic," Dad yelled.

Mom looked like she was about to toss the gravy boat at him. "Steven, please lower your voice. I get that you have questions—so do I—but you'll get nowhere with your grand inquisitor act."

"I'm sorry, Dina, but coming out this early can mean lacking the maturity to deal with the emotions and issues involved, and based on what's happened, Jeremy definitely lacks a certain maturity," Dad said, further endearing himself to me.

"Dad—" I said.

Dad shushed me with a gesture. "It's true, Jeremy. This was a very immature thing to do."

"Steven, I'm not sure I'd call it immature," Mom started to say.

Dad rolled his eyes. "Then what would you call it?"

"Since it's my life," I said, "I'd call it exploration that ended poorly, but maybe if even one of those riveting sex-ed talks had actually covered sexually transmitted diseases, perhaps I wouldn't be in this predicament—"

"Be quiet, Jeremy, this doesn't concern you," Dad said.

Goff, quiet until this time, let out a bark of cynical laughter. "Excuse me!"

Dad flushed, realizing what he'd just said. "Geoff, if you can't say anything relevant—"

"No, Steven, you can't blame that on anyone but yourself," Mom said. "What I wonder, Jeremy, is why you didn't look around at school, maybe join the GSA? That has to be full of gay kids."

Was she even for real? How would she know? "Mom, it's full of drama fags and girls looking for projects. Look at me. I'm just a normal guy. I'm not a jock. I'm not a geek. I'm not a brain. I get decent grades, and I row boats. Or did, anyway. Why do I have to fit into someone's notion of what a gay kid is?"

"Jeez, Remy, could you be more homophobic? You know I'm in the GSA. About half of those girls have brothers or sisters or aunts or uncles who're gay, bi, lesbian, or trans. And the theater crowd's kind of fun." Goff shook his head.

"Then there's the fact that most of them are straight," I said.

Goff sighed. "Okay, I have to give you that one."

"Obviously we made some mistakes, I see that," Dad said, "and at some point you locked us out, and that was your mistake. We're not the enemy here, and when you started to see us that way, you went off the rails."

I didn't say anything right away. I wasn't sure I could, because I did not want to admit I'd made a mistake, even though I had. I had the T-cell count to prove it. Mom and Dad not the enemy? Goff had been saying that for a while, and maybe to him they weren't. What none of them understood was that I had locked them out for a reason. Our parents did not understand me like they did Goff, Dad especially.

"You may not be the enemy, Dad, but you're not exactly on my side, are you?" I said, looking him straight in the eye. "After all, I was the changeling left in the cradle in place of your other, normal baby, right? The extraterrestrial dropped in your midst? Does that sound familiar, Dad?"

"I never said those words, Jeremy." The fact that Dad turned white and then dark red gave his game away.

Mom looked at Dad like she had never seen him before. "You didn't."

"I didn't think he could hear me." At least he sounded defensive. He looked anywhere but at her.

I met Goff's eyes. His mouth hung open. I had told him he and I had a different relationship with our parents—our father in particular—more times than were worth counting, but he had never believed me. I thought Goff was surprised I would say this to our parents, but then I realized that was not quite it. He was shocked I was right.

I wished I could say I felt some sense of triumph from all of this, but it just made me sad. All it really did was prove their ultimate failure as parents. Since I no longer felt like eating dry turkey or any of the sides that traditionally accompany it, let alone giving thanks for anything but a steadfast Michael or loyal brother, I left the table.

"Where do you think you're going, young man?" Dad demanded.

"I'd say to hell, but it looks like I'm already there," I called over my shoulder on my way up to my room to lie down. Maybe Michael would have his phone on him.

*

After I had woken up from a restless nap and started working on more makeup work, my parents joined me in my bedroom. This did not bode well, not if they once again presented a united face. I could deal with it. I had a few more weapons left in the arsenal, but I needed to see where this landed.

"Can we come in?" Mom said.

I put my book down. I was so far behind in AP English that it hardly mattered. "Do I have a choice?"

Dad shook his head, but Mom just put a hand on his arm. "While your father and I clearly have many things to discuss, we still need to talk to you."

Dad coughed. "Right. We're still very angry that you engaged in such dangerous activities, even if we're slowly coming to understand the reasons why you might've done so. We're also very hurt that you couldn't talk to us about something so important."

Oh, that was it, that was absolutely it. "You want to talk about that? Okay, we'll start with your compulsory heterosexuality, Mom."

"My...what?"

"Yeah, you heard me. Compulsory heterosexuality. Every time you brought up proms and told me I had to take some girl, you sent me the message loud and clear: the only thing I could be was a good little straight boy making the world better, one desperate and dateless chick at a time."

Mom looked surprised, I'll give her that much. "Remy, that's not what I meant—"

"Well, that's the message that came through." I was done, done justifying myself, done explaining the impact of their words to clueless heterosexuals. *Goddamn, if you couldn't have figured out what you were saying, then have a big bowl of shut the fuck up.*

"Jeremy, that's just not fair," Dad said. "You never told us—"

"Dad, the fair happens once a year. It's in Woodland and features rides and deep-fried I-ate-*what*-on-a-stick and unicorns crapping glitter. We're talking about my *life*." I was breathing heavily by this time. I was pissed. "Then there was your obliviousness. I tried to bring it up. I tried to tell you your stupid sex-ed talks were wrong, that I needed more, and you never *listened*."

"Rem, I'm sorry, you have no idea, but you should've been more persistent—"

"Dad, stop!" I screamed, so angry that tears ran down my cheeks. "I'm seventeen. Who's the adult? It's not my job to make you smarter."

While Dad stood there, looking on helplessly as usual, Mom braved the storm and held me, letting me cry myself out. I cried not just for their stupidity and blindness, but for myself. At last, I cried for myself.

By the time I was cried out, Dad had seated himself at my desk chair. "There's no good time to tell you this, so I'm going to get it out in the open... We—your mother and I, but mostly me—think that given everything that's going on, it's not a good idea to have you too far from home for college, at least not for the first year, maybe the first two."

That sounded bad... I lifted my head from Mom's shoulder. "You what?"

"I'm not even talking about the summer. I'm talking about how sick you've been, and the HIV you're learning to control." Dad took a deep breath. "We want you to stay locally for at least your freshman year of college, meaning either UC Davis or California Pacific."

"No." I said. "What about UC San Diego? Or BU? You can't do this to me."

Dad closed his eyes. "Please don't make this a matter of whether we can or can't because the reality is that we can. This is something we think we have to do for your health. With your grades and test scores, plus Coach Lodestone's input, you've already been accepted on early admission to California Pacific with a crew scholarship. It was a slam dunk."

I looked at my parents stupidly, like my ears were lying to me or something. "I...what?"

Mom nodded. "We know it's not what you want, and we'll talk about transferring at the end of your freshman year. For the first year, while you're learning to keep your HIV under control, you need to stay where your doctors are."

"We didn't mention your medical issues to the coach," Dad said. "We want you to know that. We only told the men's novice coach that we had personal reasons for keeping you home. We didn't say anything to her about the potential for you transferring either. That's family business."

"In essence, you'd be starting with a blank slate at California Pacific. All they know is that you've been sick and your parents want you home," Mom said.

They looked so hopeful, and I was so tired that I couldn't explode, even though that was what they deserved. I narrowed my eyes. They would pay for this one way or another. "Transfer, you say? Even to Boston University if I can get in?"

Dad flinched. "Yes, even to BU. It's the least we can do after this. I want to reiterate that this is not a punishment, although it may seem like it. Our only concern is your health at this point. We'll even write up a contract between the three of us and have it notarized."

"We're also not ignorant of the fact that your boyfriend has one more year in high school," Mom said. "This way you and Michael will still be together."

I had to hand it to them. They might have been bastards, but they were good at it. "I guess there's nothing to think about, but I need to sleep on it. I'm exhausted."

"We understand," Dad said. "Everyone in this family has a lot to process these days. I know I've been a less than ideal father, but that doesn't mean I don't love you, Jeremy, or that I'm not trying to understand."

"You've had time to get used to things, Jeremy. We've had a lot dumped on us," Mom said.

"Believe me," I said dryly. "HIV's pretty new to me too."

"Maybe this is something we can all learn about together because, Jeremy? We want you around a long time," Dad said.

"And when the time comes, we want to welcome a son-in-law to the family," Mom said.

And then Dad shocked the hell out of me. He hugged me. "Your mother's right, Jeremy. If I play my cards right, I'll come out of this with another son. If I screw this up any further, I'll lose one of the ones I have, maybe both, knowing how close you and Geoff are."

I sagged against him. Turned out, all I'd been waiting for was for Dad to say something like that.

"We'll get through this, Jeremy. I promise. I'll still say stupid things, you'll still fly off the handle, but I'll still be your father and you'll still be my son."

"And so will I," Goff said from the doorway. "Group hug?"

Which was how all four of us ended up squeezed on my bed and how my brother and I ended up sleeping there, curled up together just like when we were little kids.

*

Right after the holiday, I had another checkup with Dr. Kravitz, and my goodness was it ever embarrassing.

"You're recovered enough, and you have a boyfriend, Remy. It's time to talk about sex," Dr. Kravitz said.

My cheeks heated right up. "Um...really? Can't I just read about it?"

"How'd that work with your father's chats?" he said, peering over his glasses in that way of his.

"Uh...not so well."

"Right, then. First, we'll clear up some common misapprehensions. So, you may have heard that if you're poz, it's fine to throw condoms out and have unprotected sex with other poz men. It's called serosorting, and it's notoriously unreliable. There are multiple strains of HIV and being infected with one doesn't protect you from infection with others."

And that was news to me. "Lovely."

Dr. Kravitz nodded. "Not only that, the new strain could be resistant to your drug regimen."

"So, you can't win for losing." I sighed.

"Please don't think of it as losing. You didn't lose. You contracted a retrovirus that can be managed through medication and lifestyle decisions," Dr. Kravitz said. "No, it can't be cured yet, this is true, but you didn't lose, at life or anything else."

I snorted. "What do you call it when you end up in the hospital with blood poisoning because your immune system's taken a nosedive?"

"I call it ending up in the hospital because your immune system's taken a nosedive." Before I knew it, Dr. Kravitz took my hands between his. "I intensely hate assigning moral terms to medical issues. I saw enough of that in the '80s. It's a disease, Jeremy, not divine judgment. You're not a loser. You didn't lose. You lived, and once we figure out the right drug combination, not only will you live, you will thrive."

"It doesn't feel like it." I looked down. I still struggled with depression over this, maybe because of the crap I got at school. *What does GAY stand for? Got AIDS Yet?* I'd heard that more than once. So much for living in an ostensibly liberal community.

"I know it doesn't, not right now, but trust me. I've seen a lot of men in your position. We'll find the right combination of drugs for you, and your viral load will drop to undetectable. Do you understand what that means?"

I shook my head.

"It means that on testing, your blood and other bodily fluids will look just like everyone else's. This isn't the cure we've all been waiting for, but let me tell you, it has this old AIDS warrior's heart dancing for joy."

Dr. Kravitz squeezed my hands. He did that a lot, but I didn't mind, because right then I could see the tears in his eyes. I wondered how many patients he had lost to get to this moment. I realized it didn't matter because I knew I'd been very ungrateful. I had been given the golden ticket they had never lived to see. I would never know their names, but I had to live because they had never had the chance.

"Then HIV will feel more like a chronic condition than the death sentence it may seem right now." Dr. Kravitz pulled some flyers out of a folder. "The HIV educator was just the beginning. These are for classes about living with HIV as well as about managing your condition and the importance of your drug regimen."

I looked at them. They were a lot to take in. "These...wow."

"Yeah, wow is right. Educating yourself is critical, because eventually you'll have to educate your boyfriends, and hopefully one day a husband."

A boyfriend. "Will I be able to date? Marry? Live a normal life?"

"That's the whole point, Jeremy. This isn't the death sentence it was back in the day, but you have to believe that in here"—Dr. Kravitz pointed to his heart—"and here"—he pointed to his head. "That's what these classes are for, and what therapy is for."

"Okay then." So much to learn. I just wanted to be with Michael, not to sign up for more classes, but here it was, the ultimate AP class. If you passed the test, you got to live. When had my life become *The Hunger Games*?

Right after that first infected load hit my ass.

Something caught my eye. "What's PrEP?"

"PrEP stands for Pre-Exposure Prophylaxis," Dr. Kravitz said, "the ongoing administration of low-dose antiretrovirals to prevent infection in the sexual partners of men with HIV. It's one of the things you might need to educate your future sexual partners about. Given the ongoing nature of PrEP, it would be more appropriate for a long-term partner, as opposed to PEP, Post-Exposure Prophylaxis."

"Is that like Plan B or something?"

Dr. Kravitz chuckled. "Something like that. PEP was originally developed for medical professionals who were exposed to HIV through accidental needle sticks. An antiretroviral course started as soon as possible after exposure—"

That made sense. "That needle stick?"

"Or a condom break in your case, and it can be very effective in preventing infection. After seventy-two hours, it's worthless, however. Something to keep in mind."

More information, more overload. Dr. Kravitz wasn't exaggerating at all when he told me I had a lot to learn. I needed to learn all this before the junior prom... Michael meant everything to me, and I'd do anything to protect him. "So, if Michael and I are intimate—"

"Condoms for oral and anal," Dr. Kravitz said, handing me a card. "If a condom breaks, contact me immediately, and I mean twenty-four seven. I'll phone a prescription to a twenty-four-hour pharmacy to start PEP immediately. I won't tell you not to have sex, because we both know that's futile, but I will tell you to take all precautions necessary."

Then something occurred to me. "What about kissing?"

I wiped my hands on my pants, suddenly nervous. Before I was tested, after I got so sick, I had noticed that we hardly kissed. I missed it.

"If your boyfriend has cuts in his mouth, say from braces that tend to slice things up, or open sores, you should keep it to on the lips, but otherwise?" Dr. Kravitz shrugged. "It shouldn't be a problem."

Before, Michael and I had obliquely decided that after the junior prom we might do the deed. Now? I had no idea. Negotiated risk was one thing Michael and I had not discussed since my recovery.

"Dr. Kravitz?" I hesitated. "Can you tell me about some of them?"

"About who, Jeremy?"

"Some of the ones who didn't make it?"

Chapter Eighteen

I signed back up for weight training, hoping to speed the recovery of at least some of my previous strength. Fortunately, Dr. Kravitz and I homed in on the right drugs reasonably quickly, and the fact that I was young helped too. I still despaired of getting back in a boat for the simple reason that casual cuts and ruptured blisters meant bodily fluids everywhere. I was terrified of risking my teammates' health, but even more, I was embarrassed that I would be called out for it by those teammates. Crew meant so much to me that being sent away in shame would be more than I could ever handle. I thought it better to fade away in shame than face rejection at the hands of the sport I had devoted my life to until this point.

Besides, the weight room was proving to be difficult enough to cope with. Stephens, my old nemesis, was in my section, or maybe I was in his? Regardless, he was back and had learned some new words.

"Fuck off, leper. We don't want your kind in our weight room," he growled at me.

I groaned. "Go to hell, will you?"

"Seriously, get out of here. No one wants you or your diseases. What if you get a cut and bleed everywhere? We could get your plague."

I stood up and looked him in the eye. "The way I see it, Neanderthal, is that you'd better stay away from me. I mean, I could accidentally cut myself open like this," I said, biting my wrist. "Then what would happen to you?"

The panic on his face was hilarious, but the sentiment was not.

"All right, what's going on?"

"Coach, he's threatening to bleed on us!" Stephens said. He actually sounded scared. I had no idea ignorance still ran that rampant, and in Davis, no less. Maybe it was bussed in under affirmative action.

"Can I see you in my office, Babcock?" Coach Robertson said. I swore I heard "Badcock" as I followed him.

"Remy," Robertson said. Then he sighed. "Couldn't you just...you know, not?"

"Not what?" I said. I had an idea where this was going, but I wanted him to say it. For legal reasons. My parents had warned me about this. I think Dad had already called lawyers, just in case.

Robertson stared at me long and hard. "Do you really need to be in the weight room? You know, with your condition? Go join a gym or something."

"I don't understand what you're talking about. I've been sick and my doctor recommended weights. This section fits in my schedule." I shrugged. "I don't see what's wrong."

"That's just it. You're sick. No one wants to catch your disease." He sighed. "Maybe you could come in after hours? That's an accommodation, isn't it? We've already added bleach to the wipe-down spray bottles."

And he had just said the magic words, the words that would put the school district's collective chestnuts in a vise. I stared at him for a few minutes, and then left without saying anything. There was no point.

I cleaned up in the locker room and then sent a group text to my parents, finishing up with:

REMY: *Was this what you were waiting for?*

My dad replied with a terse *Yes*.

And within forty-eight hours, my family filed an ADA lawsuit against the school district and the city. Furthermore, our lawyer notified every major media outlet across the state, along with Lambda Legal and the ACLU. I guess it didn't matter anymore whether my parents had told the crew coach at California Pacific about my HIV or not...

*

"You know Lodestone thinks you're being silly, right?" Michael said to me one Saturday afternoon in early December. He had come to make plans for the junior prom, and it had quickly turned into making out.

"I know I'm glad you're not afraid to kiss me." I combed my fingers through his hair.

Michael looked a little shamefaced. "I'll admit I was at first, but I've done some reading. My doctor helped put my mind at ease too."

"I guess we both have things to learn about my disease," I said softly. This gave me hope for other possibilities. He *had* promised to unwrap me like a Christmas present, after all.

"Disease," Michael said, wrinkling his nose. "I've come to think of it as a condition. Anyway, Lodestone basically told me to tell you to stop kvetching and haul yourself back to practice. Time's wasting."

"He doesn't get it." I hid in the comfort of Michael's side. His summer growth spurt had clearly not finished with him. He was almost as tall as I was and definitely broader. If his joints weren't killing him, I'd be shocked, but he never complained.

"Dude, you just whined."

I sighed. "I know, but seriously. I could cut myself, and there'd be plague blood all over the place."

I couldn't see it from where I was snuggled up, but I would've bet money Michael had just rolled his eyes.

"'Plague blood,' Remy? Did you get that from *The Decameron* or *The Plague*? And I'm going to tell Lodestone you said that."

"Mean."

"No, practical. We've all discussed the matter, and we've agreed. It's time for you to get back in a boat."

We? Suddenly all my spidey senses went into full alarm, or maybe it was simple paranoia, and I sat up. "What do you mean by we? Who's we, Michael?"

"I knew that'd get your attention." Michael cackled. "Interested Parties, and that's all I'm going to say. Seriously, Remy. You're recovering physically very well," he said, glancing up and down in a way that gave me hope for that unwrapping, "but mentally? Psychologically? I'm really worried. Rowing's always been central to your world, and you've bailed on it. That can't be healthy."

I knew what he meant, I truly did. I was depressed and I knew it. I had chalked it up to a life-changing diagnosis, but what if he were right? I knew if I pulled this kind of moping where Lodestone could see me, he'd have had me on the ergs so fast I'd have gotten whiplash, if only to shut me up. The ergs did that to a body.

"Think about it, okay?" Michael said, sitting up. "In the meantime, we've got tuxes to shop for."

I tilted my head. "How much shopping is there to do, really? Tuxes are black and white. If they fit, we're golden."

"Remy, Remy, Remy." Michael sighed. He stood up. "You call yourself gay? It's a winter prom. Why should we settle for black and white when we have things like red or midnight blue or forest green to choose from?"

He yanked on my hand until I stood up.

"Let's get this over with," I said.

"Over with?"

I flinched. "Poor choice of words."

"I should think so," Michael said, leading me by the hand downstairs.

"Where are you boys headed?" Mom called.

"Shopping for tuxes!" Michael called. "Your son's hopeless."

My brother snickered from where he and Laurel were ensconced on the sofa watching a movie.

"Hopeless, huh?" I said as I got in the car. Michael might have been the alpha male, but I was the one who could drive with others in the car under California law. Legally, at any rate.

He grinned at me. "Totally."

I snorted. "We'll see about that. So where are we going, anyway? I don't think there's any place in town that rents tuxes that isn't a dry cleaner."

"And what's wrong with dry cleaning? It's made my family fairly well-off," he replied.

"Guess I stepped in that, didn't I?"

"You guess? You're in it up to your hips and sinking fast." He grinned like his meds had just kicked in.

"So, which one of your parents' shops are we going to?" I said, trying to salvage some shred of my tattered dignity.

"We're not. We're going to Nordstrom," he replied cheerfully.

I sighed. "Remind me why I put up with you, again?"

He turned in his seat and batted his eyelashes. "Because I'm cute, clever, and loyal."

"I knew there was a reason."

When I stopped at a red light, I leaned over and gave him a quick kiss.

"I'm also hung like a donkey," he said when the light turned green.

I slammed on the brakes again and almost got rear-ended—and not in the good way—for my troubles. "Don't do that while I'm driving."

His only response was wicked laughter. I was in so much trouble with him.

*

There must have been more Interested Parties than Michael let on, because when we returned to my house after looking at what was on offer, I found not only Coach Lodestone but the ladies' coach, Sabrina Littlewolf, in my living room.

I must have looked shocked because Goff laughed. "Relax, Remy. It's not an intervention."

"Actually, it is," Lodestone said. "I'm tired of your excuses and want you to come back to crew before you throw your entire senior year away."

I turned on Michael, all but shooting lasers from my eyes. "You knew about this."

"Kind of." Instead of backing away, which was what most sane people would've done, he pulled me closer. "If you think back to earlier, you'd realize why. Not rowing is killing you."

When, I wondered, had I lost control of my life? Seriously, up until Nationals, I thought I was in firm control of my destiny, or at least as much as any seventeen-year-old could be, but now? I was lucky if I got to choose my own breakfast.

"Don't be too mad at him, Remy, your parents asked me here," Lodestone said. "All Michael did was tell me your reasons, which I have to admit sounded legit to me, at least at first."

"But at least he was smart enough to talk to me," Coach Littlewolf said. She was on the short side, but I knew she had come to coaching as a former cox'n rather than as a rower. "Hello, Remy. I know we've seen each other in passing, but I don't believe we've been formally introduced. You probably already know that I'm a nurse, but what you may not know about me is that I'm in patient education for chronic diseases, and yes, that includes HIV, kiddo."

"So have a seat," Lodestone said. "I think you might be interested in what Sabrina has to say."

Littlewolf nodded and then pushed a strand of dark-brown hair behind her ear. "First of all, kudos to you for taking charge. HIV can be frightening, and it takes many people a lot longer to wake up to reality."

"It's not like I had a choice," I muttered.

"And that's where you're wrong," Littlewolf said. "A choice is exactly what you had, and you made the right one, but maybe not where crew was concerned. That's what I want to talk to you about."

I looked around and noticed that the living room had emptied of all but the rowers, no Goff or Laurel, no Mom or Dad. "Okay," I said, taking a seat, albeit somewhat hesitantly.

"How much do you know about the retrovirus?" Littlewolf said.

I took my time thinking about it and realized I didn't know all that much about HIV's natural history. Sure, I had a vague idea about how it reproduced, but mostly I'd been learning what it did to me. I said as much.

Littlewolf nodded. "I thought so. It's actually very fragile. So, if you were to cut yourself and bleed all over the place—say the tracks for the seat cut into your calves—the virus wouldn't survive very long outside of your body. That's not to say we wouldn't clean it up with a bleach solution, but that would be a simple precaution and not a public health necessity."

"But what about the oar handles? They're made of wood, and that's a porous surface," I said. "What if I develop and pop a blister? That's a body fluid, and that's what scares me."

"I can understand that, and to be honest, I hadn't thought of that possibility since the women's teams use composite handles. Again, HIV is very fragile, and while I'd have to research this to say for sure, I don't think the concentration of the virus in blister fluid—retrovirus, really—would be all that high."

But I could tell that one had stumped her.

"Those are good points, Remy," Lodestone said. "I agree that it's a concern. One solution might be to soak the handle of whatever oar you use in a bleach solution for twenty minutes or so after practice and to make sure you always use an erg with a composite grip. Another might be to buy a set of composite handles for the varsity boys' oars. They could be wiped down after every practice."

"You can buy wipes with bleach at Costco." All eyes turned to Michael, who blushed. "You can. My parents use them *everywhere*."

"So, what do you think, Remy? Would you come back if we made sure oar handles were easily washable?" Lodestone said.

I thought about it. The tracks had never been a real concern. I couldn't remember a single instance in my entire time with the Capital City junior crew that tracks had ever so much as poked at my calves, let alone dug in so deeply as to draw blood. I had only wanted to come up with any scenario I could that might involve putting other people in danger.

"I'll help you make a safety kit, Remy. It won't be too hard," Littlewolf said.

I was wavering, and they knew it. Michael had certainly read me right. Rowing definitely constituted the missing piece of my puzzle. If there was a way to row safely...

"Why don't you come back and work on your conditioning on the ergs?" Lodestone said. "That, more than anything, will tell you where you are in terms of recovery...and in terms of your teammates." When he saw my shocked look, he nodded. "Don't ever think I don't know everything that goes on with my crew. I know you've been hassled."

I looked at Michael, who looked right back at me, a hard, accusing look. "Don't you try to pin this on me. This is the first I've heard about this."

"It's only been a couple of guys," I said, suddenly tired.

"That's a few too many," Lodestone replied.

"Knock, knock," Mom said, rapping on the doorjamb. "Is this a private conversation?"

"No, not at all, Mrs. Babcock," Lodestone said. "We're just trying to talk some sense into your son."

"Good luck with that," Mom said, sitting down across the room.

Dad came in carrying a very long thin box. "Maybe this will help."

I glanced at the box and then did a double take. The label "Concept2" was displayed prominently. It was too small to contain an ergometer, which meant...

Dad set the box at my feet like a retriever and handed me a box cutter. "Open it."

I looked at Michael, but he shrugged, as in the dark as I. Then I glanced at Lodestone and noticed a very definite twinkle in his eye. Yep, a conspiracy. I must have been a bear to manage if it took this many people.

So, I opened the box. "Sculls?"

"With composite handles," Dad said. "Obviously, your mother and I had help."

Mom nodded. "You need to row, dear."

"And we're not taking no for an answer," Lodestone said.

My brother nodded. "It's not your own single, but with your own oars you won't have to worry about blisters."

"Brat," Michael muttered. "I don't have my own oars."

"So, what do you say?" Littlewolf wheedled. "Have we convinced you?"

I nodded, suddenly overwhelmed. "I'll be at practice on Monday."

"You'll start on the ergs," Lodestone said. "I'll help you set your new sculls to your measurements so you can get back in a boat over the winter break. So, what do you say?"

"Thanks, you guys." I tried not to choke up.

Lodestone nodded. "Good boy."

Chapter Nineteen

"Why're we doing this again?" I hissed at Michael without moving my lips. My cheeks hurt from faking a smile.

We stood on the stairs in my house as my parents snapped pic after pic of us dressed to the nines in our tuxedos. Technically, they were dinner jackets, but no one in these latter days knew the difference, and neither Michael nor I felt like wearing full eveningwear for the junior prom. Perhaps we would for the senior ball.

"Because your parents have been super cool about everything."

When I thought about it, I realized he was right. Mom and Dad had been troupers, at least once they got over the initial shocks to their systems. The ADA lawsuit, the ongoing issues surrounding Josh Brennan, and the elephant in the corner that was my HIV status, all of it. My smile turned more genuine.

"That's what we're looking for!" Dad exclaimed.

"Now the boutonnieres," Mom called.

We had gone through all of this at Michael's house so the Castelreighs could play paparazzi too.

"Is this why your mom insisted we buy two sets of boutonnieres?" Michael said, unpinning his from the lapels of his dinner jacket, and then waiting while I fumbled with mine. I had to be careful with the pin and all that.

I nodded as we traded boutonnieres. "By the time we're done with all this, these poor gardenias will be trashed."

"Does this count as conspicuous consumption?" he said as I pinned his to his lapel. The cameras flashed.

"Probably not."

Goff chortled. "We'll save that for the senior ball."

"Do you need to be here?" I said, glaring at him.

"Yes." Then Goff snapped some more pictures.

"Seriously, shouldn't you be at Laurel's house helping her parents hang Christmas lights?" I said. I thought that's what he was supposed to be doing.

"They'll wait for him. I had to do some fast talking to keep them from coming over," Laurel said, winking at us.

Michael and I groaned at the same time. All that produced was a chorus of "Aww, how cute."

It was so time to get out of here. I made a production of checking my cell phone. "Wow, just look at the time. We'd better jet if we're going to make our dinner reservations."

"You're not even trying to be subtle, are you?" Michael whispered.

I leaned into him to speak into his ear. I might've nibbled while I was there. "Do you want to do this anymore?"

He shuddered. "Damn, don't do that in public, and no."

"Wait there, boys. I'll be right back with the fresh flowers," Dad called as he went to the kitchen.

Michael leaned over and planted one on my cheek. Unfortunately, he damn near speared me with his hair.

"How much gel is in your hair?" I asked him.

Michael made a face. "Carcinogenic quantities. You?"

"The same."

Dad dashed up the stairs to where we stood, waiting like mannequins. He made quick work of the old boutonnieres and then handed Michael a fresh one. "Okay, Michael, first we'll take pictures of you pinning Jeremy."

I met Michael's eyes, and sure enough, the devil mouthed, "Later."

My oblivious parents took picture after picture while my smirking boyfriend attached a fresh gardenia to the lapel of my dinner jacket. I was sure people on the International Space Station could see my face, I blushed so hard. After this summer, I honestly thought I had lost the ability, but apparently, I only waited for the right man to bring it out again.

"Now it's your turn, Jeremy," Mom said.

Goff snickered. "Oh, he'll get his turn, I'm sure."

Laurel smacked his arm. I was just glad no one had said anything like "Total bottom city" or anything, regardless of whether or not it was true. *Hmmm, maybe I could get a T-shirt with that on it...*

Mom handed me the other boutonniere, and instead of making an off-color remark, I let my feelings for Michael shine through with my expression. I might have been bad at saying what I felt, but I could show him.

I took a certain satisfaction in Michael's reaction, because for once I'd made him speechless. Maybe he didn't blush like I tended to, but he looked...softer around the edges or something, and I knew he had understood.

Goff and Laurel looked at each with eyes aglow with a gimlet light. "Wait, black and white. It would capture the moment so nicely," Goff said.

Michael rolled his eyes. "How many times have they seen *Sixteen Candles*?"

"About a million. We've already worn out one DVD."

Michael's look said everything. "We can't even pay them back at the senior ball, can we?"

"No, because my parents will subject us to it all again too."

"Mine, too, if tonight was anything to go by." Michael thought about it. "Maybe we can split a limo with them."

Always practical, my Michael.

"We're leaving now," I announced to the room at large. I grabbed Michael's hand and headed for the door.

"I know you won't drink, but if you do, call. You won't get in trouble because you'll have made a smart decision," Dad called after us.

"Yes, sir!" Michael replied.

I grabbed our overcoats from the coatrack by the front door. I'd planned ahead. I knew my family, and I knew I had to be ready to make a quick getaway. I heard Goff laughing as I slammed the door behind us.

Michael slid his wool topcoat on. "Your brother laughs a lot, have you noticed?"

"He does, yes. It's a good quality to possess, isn't it?" I put my coat on, as well. December in northern California could be cold, and the stars in the clear night sky glittered like diamonds.

"I just wish it weren't always at us."

"We can't have everything." I looked at him. Damn, he was handsome. "Are you ready?"

He tucked his arm in mine and smiled at me. "Yes."

"Then your pumpkin awaits, Cinderfella."

"Why do I have to be Cinderella?"

"Cinder*fella*, and because I'm the one with a pumpkin and a license to drive it."

Michael made a frowny face. "If you're going to take that attitude—"

"When you pout like that...it's not a good look." That didn't stop me from turning him around before we got to my car and then pulling him in close. We were forehead to forehead.

"What are you going to do to make me stop frowning?" Michael said. As handsome as he was, I could have done without the baby-talk voice.

"Kiss him already!" my brother called from the dining room window.

I started to sigh, but it turned into a laugh. What else could I have done? I kissed him and made it count. Besides, I knew how to deal with straight boys. I held Michael's face between my hands and kissed him, long and hard and deep. When I felt my boyfriend's knees shake, I moved my arms, wrapping him securely, and dipped him down like that famous picture of a sailor and what was apparently a total stranger after the Second World War.

"Aww, crap," Goff said before making gagging noises.

Laurel's peal of laughter echoed across the neighborhood. "What did you expect?"

Then I heard the dining room window close. I stood Michael up, but it took a moment or two to steady him. "How was that?"

He looked a little dazed. "A very effective ploy."

"Come along, then. We have dinner reservations."

I pretended I didn't see him adjust himself.

*

The prom was fun, special because of the company rather than the clichéd "winter wonderland" theme in a high school multipurpose room. We were not the only same-sex couple there, and I'm proud to say we didn't spend the entire evening dancing in a group with the girlfriends. I was there with my boyfriend and hiding in a group with other same-sex couples was not on the agenda. Michael and I were not there to prove anything to anyone, but we were there to dance with each other, not other people. Given that my parents were already suing the school, I doubted any of the chaperones would say anything, and in any event, Michael and I weren't the type to make any public displays, our demonstration in front of my house notwithstanding.

As much fun as we had, the dance eventually ended, and I drove us back to his house. The night was still and cold around as we stood outside.

"Well?" he said.

I smiled. "Well what?"

"Don't be goofy. I've been looking forward to this for weeks. With that bow tie of yours, you look like a package—"

I snorted. "The bow's not around the package."

"You," he said, "are horrible."

"What? I didn't say you couldn't unwrap it, I just said that's not where the bow was."

Michael dragged me to the ladder. "Just for fun."

Smothering our giggles, we climbed the ladder up to his room. Form-fitting tuxes made that surprisingly difficult, but I had a feeling we wouldn't be wearing them very much longer.

He shut the window behind us and drew the blinds. Music played softly in the background: my favorite, alt-rock from the '80s on. Then he turned to me. "Well?"

"Well what?" I said again.

Michael shook his head. "You. Come here."

Then he grabbed me by the lapels of my topcoat and pulled me close. "Are you really determined to make this as difficult as possible?"

"No. Help me with my coat?"

"Turn around." I wondered if he knew just how much I liked following orders, especially his.

Divested of my coat, I helped him with his and then with his dinner jacket. Michael looked at me with his hazel eyes, and it looked to me like they held his heart. People say teens don't know anything about love, but I don't understand how they could say that. We knew what we knew with the experiences we had had. If we did not know as much as adults, it was because we had not lived as long. That did not mean we didn't feel as strongly.

"Here I am," I whispered.

He caressed my jaw and captured my lips with his, and I melted into him. He untied my bow tie and unbuttoned my shirt, one button at a time, so slowly I didn't notice until my shirt fell open and I felt his hands on my chest. Then he unbuckled my belt and, still kissing me like he owned me, he unfastened the scratchy synthetic of my rented tux pants with hands that shook just a little.

I felt him guide me back to his bed. When my knees hit the mattress, I crawled backward on it. Tall guys meant making room. "Where'd you get these moves?"

Michael grinned. "Here and there."

"I like a man of mystery." Then I noticed something. "You're wearing too much."

"I can take care of that."

I watched with hungry eyes as he slowly undressed. His eyes never left mine. For all my imagined experience, this had to be the hottest thing I'd ever seen for the simple reason that we were into each other.

Michael stood there in his underwear. "Like what you see?"

His voice dripped bravado, but we were still teenagers, and I could tell he was nervous. I swallowed the lump in my throat, suddenly full of trepidation. All I could do was nod.

He smiled and then climbed on the bed, looming over me on his knees. I pulled on his hands, bringing him down onto me, and ZOMG that felt incredible. It was the closest we had ever been and with the least amount of fabric in the way.

We both shuddered at the contact, responding immediately. My hands started roaming, but Michael growled in my ear. I shook under him, vulnerable and wanting and desperate.

"No," he said, his voice raspy. He grabbed my hands and pulled them over my head. Transferring them to one hand, he reached out and turned off the light by his bed. "Tonight, you're mine and you'll do what I say."

"How did you know?" I whispered.

It was moments before he spoke. "You've told me in a hundred little ways."

"Is that okay?" I had never felt more exposed in my entire life. It scared me. It thrilled me.

"Listen to me, Remy... Jeremy," he said roughly, taking my jaw in his free hand. He had never called me by my full name, and I stilled at his touch. "I need it too. You taught me that."

And then he claimed me. We claimed each other.

I woke up later, early in the morning. Music still played in the background. Irony of ironies, LaTour's "People Are Still Having Sex." Interestingly enough, the lyrics were different from the CD I had at home, instead of "this AIDS thing's not working," it was "this safe thing's not working." The thing of it was, safe would have worked, at least for me. If I had received the information in time. If my partners had said something. If I had thought with the big head.

Curious, indeed. The lyrics let me know that on some level, despite all the mistakes I had made, my need for sexual contact was a natural one. People needed to be touched, and no matter what kind of message society sent, people would always seek out the touch they needed. So no, this AIDS thing wouldn't and didn't stop it, not in the West among gay men and not in Africa among heterosexuals.

Last spring, I had wanted that touch from Michael. He had wanted to give me that touch. We had both been confused and hadn't known how to do it. Maybe I should have tried harder to make him see. No maybe about it, actually, but I hadn't, and that oar's puddle had passed the stern deck and disappeared. It was time to worry about the next stroke. We were here now, and that was what mattered.

That was what I loved about crew. Every stroke was another chance to do it right, an entire sport devoted to do-overs. That thing you had just done wrong? That was old news. Lesson learned, forget it, and move on.

So yeah, I had sought out the touch of others, and it hadn't gone so well. That didn't mean I had been wrong to have done so. It meant I had gone about it the wrong way. I had flown the nest a little sooner than I should have. It meant I had thought I was a little more grown-up than I really was. That was all. I flew back, wings singed, lesson learned.

Michael and I had ended up together, after all. Who knew what the future would bring us? I started college next year. Michael had one more year of high school. For now, we were together. I hoped we would stay that way, but we both faced a lot more growing up. I knew one thing: he would always be my friend.

Epilogue

APRIL
My senior year

This was it, the last race of my high school rowing career. In seven minutes or so, I would finish my time with the Capital City Rowing Club junior crew and hand it all over to Michael. I couldn't think of better hands. They'd certainly handled me well. Damn, so not the thought to have when I wore nothing but form-fitting Spandex and a tight jockstrap. Then it would all be over but the postmortem and the goodbyes. I was proud of my time with Cap City, for all its ups and downs. I had grown up on the crew, and I had made some lifelong friends. Some I had already said goodbye to, some I hoped would accompany me through life. But right then was not the time to dwell on my sorrows and my joys. We had finished our warm-up row on the ass end of Mission Bay, and it was time to get my head in the boat.

"Good luck," I said, reaching a fist back to seven. Right then, he was no more than my seven seat, even if on shore he was my smoking-hot boyfriend.

"Good luck," Michael said, bumping his fist into mine before he turned around and repeated the ritual with six seat, and so on down the boat.

I was in my zone, sensory input flowing in and out of my consciousness but not lingering. I responded but didn't react.

Howie, the cox'n, called low-voiced commands to bow and two to correct the boat's trajectory in our lane. Not my problem. That responsibility lay with Howie and the kid in the stake boat holding our stern. If they needed me to do anything, they would tell me.

"We have alignment."

"Ready all," Howie said softly.

We were already at our catch position, the blades of the oar buried in the water. I wiggled my fingers on the oar's composite handle to avoid a death grip. Those led to blisters and were indicative of sloppy technique.

The starter's horn shattered the silence of the starting line.

"Row!" Howie barked into his microphone. *Git, y'all!*

Eight rowers moved as one through the starting sequence to break inertia's hold on the *Helena Sundstrom*.

Half!

Three-quarters!

Half! Half!

Full! Full!

"Twenty high!" bellowed Howie.

By that time, the *Helena* flew across the calm water of Mission Bay.

So did the hulls of the other crews, and we were not the fastest.

I knew only the world before my eyes, the steely-eyed glare that was the determination of Howie Chen.

"Three boat lengths to the Little Knights," Howie barked. "How badly do you want this? Show me!"

A short man on dry land, he spoke with the voice of a titan in the boat.

"Five hundred meters in. Big legs, this stroke." He would be all but voiceless by the end of the race, but right now, his voice was our world.

"Focus thirty. Now."

So, we focused. Our bodies burned. But I knew I lacked that essential fire I had summoned at the Nationals, that fury that had made me consume myself. Where had it gone?

"We've barely moved on the Little Knights. Halfway through the race and they're holding us off. What are you waiting for?" Howie yelled. "Bring your focus into the boat. Not what you're going to do at the end of the race, fuck that. Right here, right now. Ratio shift, in two."

That was me. I was stroke. They were rushing me, and I would slow them down. Me and Michael.

"Let's do...this," I huffed to Michael.

Howie smiled. "That was one...and two."

And we did it, Michael and I. We stood on our foot stretchers and pulled our blades through the water faster and took just a bit longer on our recovery.

"That's it, men. That's what I want to see...and we just took a seat on the Little Knights. Do it again. Then gimme that focus thirty."

Slowly but surely, we started to walk up on them as Howie counted off the strokes.

"Less than a boat length," Howie said tersely. "Show them how we row at Cap City."

We didn't have that much time left. I couldn't look, but I knew Howie's expressions—he looked super intent. That meant we were close, damn close.

His eyes lit up. "*Bow ball!*"

That wasn't for us. That was for them, just to psych them out.

"Up two in two," he all but whispered, his voice caressing us. "One...and two."

So, Michael and I took the pace up, the six behind us backing us every breath and stroke.

The *Helena* flew once again.

So focused had we been on the Little Knights that we had never seen the other boats, and that was probably Howie's strategy. By the time I saw the buoy indicating the final five hundred meters, it was only Cap City and the Little Knights.

"We're half a boat length ahead of them. Are we going to make a move or not?" Howie said tightly. He looked straight through me and the rest of us to the finish line. He carefully glanced to the side and behind. "They're starting. They know they have to if they're going to pull this out. This is the finals. Bring it up now. Empty the fucking tank or lose. You choose."

To our credit, we kept it smooth, no panicked flailing, just a measured increase, step by step, beat by beat. I had found that fire at long last, and it was a pleasure to burn.

I heard screaming on the shore, but I didn't care. Step by step, stroke by stroke. I could almost—but not quite—sense another boat out of the corner of my eye. "Now!"

"You heard him! All of it!" Howie screamed. "You can puke when we're done."

Cap City! Cap City! Cap City!

Then an air horn's wail, and again almost immediately.

"Way enough! Oars down," Howie rasped, his voice barely above a whisper. "All eight, check it down."

With a flick of our wrists, we turned the blades of our oars from parallel to the water's surface to perpendicular and stabbed them into Mission Bay, halting the momentum of our boat.

And it was over.

Acknowledgements

As always, I'm happy to thank my former coach, Tricia Blocher, for knowing the fiddly rowing details I don't. Likewise, Whitney Powell, a brilliant cox'n, helped me with crucial information about high school rowers applying for college and early admissions for athletes. Chillbear, as he always does, helped me with police procedural details without asking me too many questions. Any errors belong to me, not him.

No writer can ever let acknowledgments slide by without thanking his beta readers. As always, my husband read over my manuscript with careful attention to detail, but I get to thank Posy Roberts and Brandilyn too. *Poz* also went into a gamma round, so thanks, too, to Becky Condit. *Poz* was in great hands with these four.

Thank you, too, to the folks at NineStar: Rae, my publisher; Elizabeth, my editor who's been a dream to work with; Natasha, whose covers make these guys come alive; and the unnamed proofreaders who catch mistakes that have survived too many rounds of editing.

About C. Koehler

Christopher Koehler always wanted to write, but it wasn't until his grad school years that he realized writing was how he wanted to spend his life. Long something of a hothouse flower, he's been lucky to be surrounded by people who encouraged that, especially his long-suffering husband of twenty-nine years and counting.

He loves many genres of fiction and nonfiction, but he's especially fond of romances, because it's in them that human emotions and relations, at least most of the ones fit to be discussed publicly, are laid bare.

While writing is his passion and his life, when he's not doing that, he's a househusband, at-home dad, and oarsman with a slightly disturbing interest in manners and the other ways people behave badly.

Christopher is approaching the tenth anniversary of publication and has been fortunate to be recognized for his writing, including by the American Library Association, which named *Poz* a 2016 Recommended Title.

E-mail
christoarpher@gmail.com

Facebook
www.fb.me/Christopher.tells.stories

Twitter
@christopherink

Website
www.christopherkoehler.net/blog

Other NineStar books by this author

CalPac Crew series
Rocking the Boat
Tipping the Balance
Burning It Down
Settling the Score

Coming Soon from C. Koehler

All That Is Solid Melts into Air

The Lives of Remy and Michael, Book Two

So far, I'd made it halfway through the first semester of my freshman year at California Pacific, and you know? I had to admit that it didn't suck. I know, I know, that was a bizarro thing to say about one's choice of school, but there's something you have to remember. CalPac was most assuredly not my choice of school. I made some very...I'll call them colorful...choices the summer before my senior year of high school, and the gods of indiscriminate love rewarded me with HIV. It almost killed me—mostly because I neither told anyone but my brother and my boyfriend, nor did I seek medical care—but my parents made a decision that I resented at the time: rather than sending me across the country to Boston University, they spoke to the men's crew coach at CalPac. Between their persuasion and some fast talking from my high school coach, the ever-awesome Peter Lodestone, I wound up going to the local private university in the Sacramento area with a full-ride scholarship so long as I stayed brilliant in the boats. Mom and Dad's idea was that I spend my first year in college at CalPac as I learned to quote, unquote manage my condition, and at the end of that we'd discuss transferring.

I flipped out when they dropped this bomb on me, and I dropped an R-bomb on them in return. R-bombs. That's what Michael affectionately called my rages. They're like daisy cutter cluster bombs but involved words and caused a lot more damage. All my plans—all *our* plans, as Michael and I had our future worked out—gone, just like that. But my parents knew me well, surprisingly enough, or at least knew my temper, and to take the sting out of it, they made a contract with me: in return for my cooperation, they gave me a notarized promise that at the end of my freshman year I could transfer to the school of my choice. Or maybe the school of my choice that chose me back might be a better way to phrase it. At the time I felt so sure of my future. Row my seat, keep my grades up at CalPac while I applied to BU, and bide my time while Michael finished high school. As soon as he graduated, I'd transfer so fast people behind me would get pneumonia from the wind in my wake. Michael and I would stay on the same schedule on the East Coast. That was the Plan. I'd worry about NCAA eligibility later.

Oh, and then there was my father's edict that despite the fact they lived across the Yolo Causeway from CalPac, I would live in the dorms. That went over well.

"You've got to make the break, Remy," my dad had said.

As I recall, I made a face. "Dad, no. I'll be what, fifteen miles from home? How much of a break could I possibly make?"

"Trust me." Dad snorted. I remembered that clearly. "Once you're there you'll realize we might as well be on the moon. It'll seem like a world away, and one more thing—you can come home *maybe* once in a while, but under no circumstances will your mother and I allow you to come every weekend."

"What? Why not?" I think I whined.

Then Mom jumped in. "That seems a bit harsh, Steven."

"He'll never make the transition to any kind of independence if he does, Dina. He'll be more likely to drop out, and he's too good a student to allow that. I can show you the research, if you want."

"There's research?" Mom had sounded surprised, and I didn't blame her. Dad could be autocratic sometimes.

I still saw Dad nodding. "You bet there is, hon. This isn't me being arbitrary, for once."

"Then I agree," Mom had pronounced before turning to me. "We want you to stay close to home to make sure you learn what you need to know about your HIV from Dr. Kravitz, not to create a state of permanent dependency."

So, there I was at CalPac and living in the dorms. There was one thing I was absolutely unprepared for when I agreed to all of this with my parents.

I loved CalPac.

Also from NineStar Press

Rocking the Boat by C. Koehler

Nick Bedford coaches the men's rowing team at California Pacific College, a small liberal arts school in Sacramento. He's quiet, dedicated—and closeted. He struggles with professional ethics and NCAA rules as he denies his attraction for Morgan Estrada, one of his rowers. While they may not be far apart in age, the difference between coach and athlete leads Nick to worry about exploitation.

But Morgan has desires and a mind of his own, and what he wants is his coach. As the spring racing season advances, Morgan feels his coach's eyes on him. Morgan may be gay, and while he's not out to team, he hasn't hidden it, either. It may be a coach's job to check out an athlete's form, but Morgan hopes Nick's interested in more than his technique.

Morgan corners Nick in the boathouse, and Nick admits that while he wants Morgan he can't have him. Morgan laughingly points out that he's not bound by any of those rules and he wants Nick. Nick and Morgan start a relationship, but Nick worries whenever they're in public: what if someone sees? An anonymous complaint from a rower to the athletics director sends Nick's worries into overdrive just as the crew prepares for the make-or-break race of the year.

The Couple Next Door by Rick R. Reed

Jeremy Booth leads a simple life, scraping by in the gay neighborhood of Seattle, never letting his lack of material things get him down. But the one thing he really wants—someone to love—seems elusive. Until the couple next door moves in and Jeremy sees the man of his dreams, Shane McCallister, pushed down the stairs by a brute named Cole.

Jeremy would never go after another man's boyfriend, so he reaches out to Shane in friendship while suppressing his feelings of attraction. But the feeling of something being off only begins with Cole being a hard-fisted bully—

it ends with him seeming to be different people at different times. Some days, Cole is the mild-mannered John and then, one night in a bar, he's the sassy and vivacious drag queen Vera.

So how can Jeremy rescue the man of his dreams from a situation that seems to get crazier and more dangerous by the day? By getting close to the couple next door, Jeremy not only puts a potential love in jeopardy, but eventually his very life.

The Silence of Lightning
by Maries S. Crosswell

Former pro-rodeo champion Smith Rose and his cousins Cooper and Christa Boone live a quiet life together in the town of Cody, Wyoming—until the summer of 2015 shakes them to their foundations.

Stuck in an unhappy rut since his retirement from the rodeo five years prior, Smith is forced to reckon with his past, present, and future when his former friend and lover John Henry Walker shows up at Smith's bar. Meanwhile, the Boone sisters face a threat they never would've predicted when an out-of-town stranger begins to stalk

Christa after meeting her at a party. While trying to support her sister and their cousin, Cooper secretly agonizes over her fears of their little family splitting apart and where that would leave her.

When Smith, Cooper, and Christa's problems converge in a dangerous confrontation, will the three of them survive?

Connect with NineStar Press

www.ninestarpress.com

www.facebook.com/ninestarpress

www.facebook.com/groups/NineStarNiche

www.twitter.com/ninestarpress

www.instagram.com/ninestarpress